THE PRINCE RETURNS

KEEPER OF DRAGONS

BOOK 1

J.A. Culican

Edited by: Danielle Carioti

Cover Art by: Christian Bentulan

ISBN: 978-1533469380

www.dragonrealmpress.com

For my youngest daughter, Eva and her love of all things magical.

J.A. Culican

Contents

J.A. Culican

Prologue

I slammed the front door behind me and kicked off my shoes towards the closet. My mom constantly yelled at me for not putting my shoes where they belonged, but I couldn't be bothered today. My job search for anything came up empty once again. I graduated high school a month ago and had searched day in and day out for anything I could do to occupy my time. College was out of the question, my grades were barely mediocre and I had little talent elsewhere, so no schools knocked on my door when scholarship time came. All in all, I was close to hating life these days. I had sat back and watched all of my classmates talk about their grand post-high school plans and how excited they were to attend colleges. On my side of things- I had nothing going. And while all through high school, nothing was glorious and free, right now, "nothing" felt like a black hole, where I would disappear forever.

"Cole, come have a seat. Your mother and I have something important to talk to you about." My dad directed from the other room. His voice sounded serious.

I wasn't in the mood for whatever my parents had to talk to me about, I wanted to ignore my dad's command, but something in his voice had me concerned. I stepped into the living room and plopped down on the old recliner. Sooner or later I thought for sure I would plop and hit the floor with all the groans and creaks the chair made. My dad had refused time and time again to get rid of it. I looked up at my parents as they sat across from me on the old rickety couch. They looked...scared? What could they possibly be scared about?

"Cole," my mom started and hesitated, she looked at my dad, lowered her head, and started to cry.

"Mom, dad what's going on? Is everything okay?" I started to shake as I spoke, unsure of what was about to happen. I had never seen my mom so frightened before. "Is everything okay?"

My dad took a deep breath, "Cole, the last few days have been hard for your mom and me." He paused and grabbed my mom's hand. "I'm disappointed in myself. We let our fear lead us as we raised you. We were so worried someone would find out about you. We never pushed you to do anything, we completely sheltered you from everything." He let go of my mom's hand and put his arm around her shoulders. He squeezed as she continued to cry.

I was confused, I hadn't realized they were that disappointed in me. "I'm sorry dad, I really..."

My dad raised his free hand in my direction, in an attempt to wave off my response. "No, Cole just listen, let me finish." He declared. "Cole, your mother and I always wanted a family. Unfortunately, we weren't able to. That was until you." He paused and took a breath, beside him my mom nodded her head in silence. He continued, "You were our miracle, our chance at being whole." He explained.

"Dad, I don't understand." I shook my head in confusion. "I know all this, so why do you both look so frightened?" I had heard the story a million times about how thankful they were for me, how they had tried for years to have children and were unsuccessful.

My dad continued. "Cole, you came to us...when you were just a small baby." His voice wavered as he stared at me with a look of uncertainty.

Wait, what? I felt uneasy. A nervous sensation engulfed me and didn't leave for quite some time. It felt like a dark, gloomy cloud that lurks in the sky on a rainy day. But a rainy day I don't question. This I questioned.

"Are you saying I was adopted?" I began to fidget in my seat as I digested what my parents were trying to tell me. I clasped my hands on my lap to stop the tremble that had begun to take over my body. "Why wouldn't you tell me this before? I mean kids are adopted all the time." I started to ramble, but I couldn't help it. I began to feel angry at them, why would they keep this a secret? How didn't I know? Okay, I was adopted, but why did they both look so scared as they told me this fact? Did they think I would leave or go look for my biological parents? That was a thought I was not ready to deal with.

Letting go of my mom, my dad held his hands up to stop my rambling, "Let me finish Cole. Your mother and I, we love you as if you were our own. To us, you are ours and always have been and always will be."

This I knew, since I had no clue they weren't my real parents, until now. They had proven their love for me over and over throughout the years, but this thought didn't stop the anger I felt towards them. I couldn't grasp why they would keep this from me.

"We honestly never thought we would be given the chance to have a baby, but then your parents came to us," my dad gave me a look of doubt.

"Wait, you met them?" I couldn't believe it. My hands began to lose circulation from the grip I had on them. I released my hands and shook them out as my mind raced further. "Do you know them? Do I? Why'd they give me up?" I started to babble again, it was like I couldn't get my thoughts straight. My mood jumped around just as much as my thoughts. I was mad one second and scared the next.

"Your biological parents love you just as much as we do. That's why they gave you to us. They trusted us to raise you and love you as our own."

Now I was confused, my brain couldn't even ramble this time, even the nerves that shook my body stopped. I was frozen as I sat there and stared at the two people in my life who had always been my home.

"We made a promise to them. We promised..." My dad paused, and looked at my mom. She hadn't taken her eyes off me, almost like she thought I was going to just up and disappear. My dad finally turned back to me, "We promised to give you back when you turned eighteen."

"But, but that's like... in two days?" I stuttered as I gaped at my parents. I was so confused and a little alarmed by the short notice. They were just going to what, hand me over to two people I had never met? Then what? I began to panic.

My dad stood up and came over to me, he grabbed me under my chin, which forced me to look him in the eyes. "It was part of our promise, we couldn't tell you until it was time. You're special Cole, and your family, they're protectors, just as you will be." He stated. "I know your mother and I have just dumped a lot of information on you, and I am really sorry Cole. We had hoped we would have more time. But we don't."

Protectors? How am I supposed to be a protector? And a protector of what? I could barely take care of myself. My mom did everything for me; cooked my meals, cleaned my laundry...she even made my bed for me each morning. My mind raced with questions, but I couldn't get a single one out. I was confused, frightened, and even angry. I wasn't sure which emotion was most dominant at the moment. I could only imagine what kind of expression I had on my face. We sat in silence as the minutes passed by, our thoughts kept to ourselves.

Finally, my dad broke the silence, "Cole, it's getting late. Why don't you head to bed, and we will talk more tomorrow. Let everything sink in, get your thoughts straight. I know this is hard, but I promise it will be alright." My dad reached for my elbows to prop me up. As soon as I was on my feet my mom rushed over and threw her arms around me, my body stiffened from her contact.

"I love you Cole, no matter what." She whispered in my ear as my body began to relax in her hold.

After she let me go, I turned and ran up the stairs to my room. I shut my door, ambled over to my bed and sat down. My thoughts were still all over the place, an internal uproar flurried in my head. I only knew one thing for sure, there was no way I would get any sleep that night.

Chapter One

Two hours and thirty-one minutes. That was all the time I had left before my real parents were scheduled to arrive. My thoughts weren't any clearer now than when my parents sat me down two nights ago. The questions I had, I received no answers to. It seemed my *parents* took me in on faith and faith alone. They never questioned why they were given me or why I had to be given back at eighteen. I attempted to talk with my mom the next morning at breakfast after news broke of my imminent departure. *"Coley we wanted you so bad, it didn't matter the why, we loved you immediately,"* that was the only reason I got from my mom. I didn't push further, as soon as she called me Coley, a name she hadn't used since I was little, I knew she was hurting. Her voice trembled as she spoke, it made me think she was scared. Which, in turn, made me scared. I stopped with the questions and went back to my room.

I've spent the last two days holed up in my room with my cell phone turned off. My friends wouldn't understand. How could they? I didn't even understand what was going on. What would I even say to them? Everyone was busy getting ready to leave for college anyway. Me, I had no plans, but *I guess I did now.*

I figured this, once I got settled at where I was headed, I'd give them a call and we could all have a good laugh over it. At least that's what I banked on. My closest friend Eva had left for college a few weeks earlier, I remember she had mentioned something about summer classes. She was the only one who tried to get me to apply to college or, at least make a plan. She was unsuccessful, so here I sat. I hadn't heard from her in a few weeks, I hope the distance didn't pull us apart, she's my one and only friend I could always count on.

Eva was the one person who I had always trusted. Since the day she moved in with her grandparents next door, we were inseparable. That was almost eight years ago. Besides my parents, she was the only other person who got me, and accepted me. I guess I just never fit in anywhere, not athletic or smart, just average. Average everything right down to the way I looked. I had never been anything special, which was fine by me, it kept me out of the spotlight and behind the scenes, right where I felt comfortable. Eva on the other hand, I had no doubt would do great things, she was beautiful and smart. The girl could talk circles around me. I was definitely going to miss her.

Of all things, the whereabouts of my new home had bothered me the most; my imagination and maybe my lack of sleep hadn't helped. Whenever I dared to close my eyes, outrageous visions of a place I had no name for filled my head. It made me feel like I was flying in an airplane. All I could see were clouds, but there was something special about those clouds. They almost looked like they were painted, too perfect to be real. The vision was so close, I almost felt like I was there. A noise outside my door startled me out of my daydream.

"Cole," my Dad's voice sounded strange, "Can I come in?" He seemed worried, like I would actually tell him "no."

I got up off my bed to walk across my room and open the door. There stood my dad, hunched over. He looked...defeated? Instantly, my panic came back. I stepped backwards to let my dad in. He entered and took my spot on the bed I just vacated. Only then did I notice my bed was unmade, my plain blue comforter was smooshed at the bottom of my bed in a ball. My mom hadn't been in today to make it like she always did.

My thoughts quickly moved to my dad after I realized he hadn't said anything yet. He held his head in his hands and stared at the ground. He looked like he was going to say something, but changed his mind. Finally, after what felt like minutes, though really just a few seconds, he looked up at me. "Cole, no matter what, I just want you to know you always have a home here. You will always be our son." He rushed all this out on one single sob.

He continued to stare at me as tears fell from his eyes. I had no idea what I was supposed to say to that. I know I was confused about, well, just about everything. But I never questioned their love for me or that they wanted to hand me over or that they were kicking me out.

Now that I had heard it straight from my dad, it hit me hard. I would always see him as my dad, but I now had another dad. A dad who I didn't know at all, who gave me away as a baby, who I was just supposed to...accept? How did this thought never escape my mind the last two days? It was like all I had thought about was where I was going, and who my real parents were. It seemed like I basically had no choice but to accept this fate. But I did have a choice. *Right?* I mean I was eighteen, a legal adult, I could stay.

My Dad continued to stare at me; he was waiting for some sort of reply. My thoughts had taken over again and I forgot for a moment he was there. "Dad,

I don't have to leave. I'm an adult now. Tonight when my biological parents come by, I can meet them and send them on their way. Nothing has to change." I was holding my breath, awaiting his reply. Whatever he said next could change everything.

I could barely hear him when he responded, "I wish that were true, your mother and I would want nothing more than to have you stay here with us, forever." The pain in his voice was almost unbearable. "Yes, you're now a legal adult, but I fear where you're going, your age won't make a difference." He stopped and sucked in a breath, almost like he wasn't supposed to tell me any of that.

Wait, did he say my age wouldn't matter where I was going? But I thought, "What do you mean?" I didn't mean to say this out loud, but I did. My father flinched. "I thought you didn't know where I was going?" Nothing else could come out of my mouth, I just looked at him while I waited for a response. *Maybe I heard him wrong?*

He looked uncomfortable. "I'm so sorry Cole. I just, I just need you to trust me. Promise me you will go with them tonight without a fight. Keep an open mind. Your mom and I love you so much. We want nothing but the best for you, and this is the best." I could tell each word that passed his mouth was more painful than the last. He looked like he was in complete agony.

I was more confused now than before he came up the stairs. I just wanted this all to be over. For someone to answer my questions. Nothing made sense at all.

My dad interrupted my inner debate, "Please, come downstairs and have dinner with your mom and me. Please, we…" He couldn't finish his thought, I could tell he felt beaten.

"Yeah…I'll be down." For some reason, I couldn't be mad at him, it was clear he didn't want any of this to happen. I just wished he would answer my questions. He seemed to know more than he initially let on.

He stood up to leave my room, and looked back at me when he reached the doorway. "I love you Cole, no matter what, remember that." With that, he walked out and quietly closed the door behind him. An ominous feeling was left behind with his parting words.

I wasn't sure how dinner was going to go, but I decided if I had to leave tonight, I didn't want to leave on a bad note. My parents, even with everything that had happened in the last two days, had always been the best parents anyone could ever ask for. That is the one thing I could be grateful for. At least my birth parents had left me with a couple who loved and cared for me better than any other parent could. They had always supported me in everything. I never would have thought I wasn't biologically theirs. It was this thought alone that propelled me from my room to head down for dinner. My parents deserved everything I could give them. Everything in my life was because of them, and I wouldn't let them down.

As I made my way down the stairs and into the kitchen, I could hear my parents as they talked in hushed voices to each other. I wasn't sure if I should wait a few minutes and let them finish their quiet conversation or just head in. I guessed my dad was letting my mom know how his talk had just went with me. I wondered if he thought it was successful or not? To be honest, I wasn't sure what to think about anything anymore.

Finally, I found the courage and walked into the kitchen. As soon as I walked in, both of my parents turned and looked at me. My mom had a relieved expression on her face. *Did they think I wouldn't show?* It took me a second to collect my bearings; I walked over to the table and had a seat in the same chair I had sat in for the last eighteen years, almost every night for dinner. Rarely did we eat anywhere else except this table, my mom always insisted we eat as a family every night. *This might be our last family dinner.* That thought alone depressed me.

My parents headed over to the table carrying various plates of food. When I looked at the assorted plates on the table I noticed my mom had made my favorite dinner, corned beef hash. Eva once told me this was a favorite meal amongst Texans, but I guess I wouldn't know. I had never left the great state of Texas, I only left the small town of Clover a few times. It was the town where everyone knew everyone. The kids here were dying to leave, with not much here and all. College was one of the few ways out, but I guess I never had the need to flee like everyone else. *Again, my mind rambled.*

My mom interrupted my thoughts, "Happy Birthday Cole."

I could tell she was trying to sound cheerful when she said this. I had completely forgotten today was my birthday. Usually turning eighteen is all teens could think about. I guess the whole being sent back to wherever I came from on this day, to protect something I didn't know, took away the happy excitement I should have felt. I finally looked up at my mom and mumble a thank you. I could tell she wanted to say more, but stayed quiet, gesturing for me to eat. I started to eat, not tasting anything. I was sure it all tasted wonderful like it always did. My mom was one of the best cooks I knew. But then I wondered if my real mom knew how to cook? *I guess I would find out soon.*

Once I cleared my plate, my mom brought out an apple pie, again one of my favorites. I knew it was my birthday and she just wanted to make me happy, but it was getting to be too much. It made me think of all the things I was going to miss.

"I don't want to go!" I blurted out.

My parents looked at me with a look of regret, maybe pity. All these emotions in the last few days overwhelmed me. My dad came around the table and kneeled next to me. "We know son, and we don't want you to go either, but it's what has to happen." He took my hand and pulled me up, "Come on, let's go watch some of that horrible reality TV you like so much, we have a little bit of time before your parents arrive." His voice seemed caught on the word parents, but he continued to pull me to the living room as though nothing he just said hurt him at all.

Thanks for the reminder Dad. I knew he just wanted to get my mind off everything. Maybe he was right, mindless TV sounded okay. I started to walk with him. I made it about two steps before I began to feel strange. It was like my whole body was pulsating with some kind of energy. I tried to look to my dad for some kind of confirmation that he was feeling it too, but he looked blurry, like I was looking at him through a film. The vibration started to intensify, I wasn't sure how much more I could take. I attempted to say something, but all I could manage was some kind of whimper. I thought my parents were speaking to me, but I couldn't be sure, nothing made sense, my legs gave out, and a crazy energy started to devour me. Suddenly, everything went silent.

Chapter Two

A loud bang echoed through my head. All I wanted to do was cover my ears, but my arms weren't cooperating. My parents were next to me, I could feel them as they grabbed at my arms. *Were they moving me?* I could hear a shriek of sorts, but everything was foggy, so I couldn't make out exactly what was being yelled, or who was yelling it.

Without warning, the energy that pulsed through me stopped. It caught me off guard, I couldn't catch my breath for a moment. Everything that had just happened came back to me. I looked up to find my mom staring down at me, I thought my dad was here, but I couldn't see him. Somehow I had managed to find myself on the old green couch in the living room. "Mom..." I squeaked out.

She looked at me with concern; she was just as confused as me about what had happened. "Just stay still Cole, I'm sure everything is going to be okay."

She looked over the couch at something behind me, *maybe my dad?* I looked closer at her face, she looked pale. I guess the last few days had been rough on everyone, not just me.

My mom took a deep breath and looked back down at me. With a look of astonishment, she whispered, "Your parents are here, your dad is in the other room with them. I'm not sure how long he is going to be able to keep them out."

How long had I been out of it? It had felt like mere minutes. We still had a good half hour until my parents were supposed to arrive. I tried to sit up but was unsuccessful, so my mom helped me. She sat next to me with her arm around me, neither of us said a thing. I was glad she was there, without her support, I would've gone completely crazy.

The door that separates the living room and foyer banged open, I twisted on the couch to look behind me. In walked a massive man who looked to be about thirty-five. He crouched his neck and shoulders as he entered through the door, he was well over six feet tall. I'm not sure I had ever seen a man of this size, I became instantly alert. Behind him was a woman about the same age, she was beautiful. She had long golden hair and a perfect complexion. She wasn't much shorter than the massive man standing in front of her. My dad stood behind them. He looked so small, and seemed a little intimidated by our visitors.

The man was the first to speak. "My son, how are you feeling? I did not expect our power to affect you in the manner it did." He walked closer to us as he spoke. He regarded me in a predatory manner, it took everything I had not to get up and run out of the room. He stopped in front of my dad's recliner and looked down at me, waiting for a response.

I couldn't get my mouth to work, thankfully my mom saved me. "Rylan, Sila please come in and have a seat." She pointed to the recliner across from us. "The two of you haven't changed at all since the last time we saw each other, hard to believe it's been eighteen years already."

There was no way these two could be my parents. They looked way too young, and the more I observed, nothing like me. The man's hair was a dark shade of red, which I knew only a few people could get away with; on him, dark red looked strong and powerful. The woman had an impressive head of golden blonde locks, which I found odd because I had a dull shade of brown for hair. Not to mention their eyes, they both had the same shade of jade green. I was completely mesmerized, the color had a calming effect as they shined like emeralds. My eyes were a wonderful shade of mud. How was any of this even possible? *I did pay attention a little in biology class.*

Rylan, my *father*, looked from my mom to me, nodded his head and advanced towards my dad's favorite recliner. He plunked down on it and the predictable creaks and groans ensued. I held my breath as I waited for the chair to crumble to the ground under the behemoth sitting in it. Sila, my *mother* joined him, she stood behind the recliner and faced my mom and me. I was thankful when my dad joined us on the couch, he sandwiched me between them. I sent a silent prayer up for the support they had continued to give me.

All the attention was now on me, I hadn't uttered a single word throughout the whole exchange, and I had nothing to add, even now. I sat nestled between my parents while I stared at the two people who wanted to take me from my home.

"What's the plan from here?" My dad's voice rang through the silent air. It seemed extremely loud after the intense silence. My Dad cleared his throat and looked around, "I mean, Cole just found out that the two of you existed. He has a lot of questions we haven't been able to answer."

"There will be time later to answer all your questions," Rylan looked only at me as he spoke. "We must be going, we only have the cover of night for so many hours, and we have quite some distance to cover. Do not worry Michael," he finally turned away from me and focused on my dad. "You will be compensated for taking care of our son. Our people will forever be grateful for you and Ella."

Well that news got my adrenaline to spike. This guy was crazy if he thought I was just going to get up and walk out, without so much of an introduction from him or the woman standing behind him. Especially after the mention of "our people." What people?

In true Cole fashion I blurted out the first thing that came to my brain. "No way, I don't want to go anywhere with you." This could go well, after all, I spoke only the truth.

This time, the woman, Sila answered, "Son, we know you don't understand what is going on, but everything will make sense once we get you home," she assured me. "We will have all the time in the world to answer your questions. But, like your father said, we don't have the luxury to sit here and discuss this further." Just like her eyes, Sila's voice seemed to soothe my nerves, too. I started to stand without a thought. I got all the way to the door before my brain started to kick in again. *What had just happened?*

I turned and looked at everyone in the room, Rylan had already stood from the recliner. I was so confused. I mean there was no way I was going with them! Why did I just leave the comfort of my parents? I wanted nothing more than to run back over and jump between them and stay there forever. But now that I was up, I needed to play this just right, maybe I could make a run for the front door? Or run up to my room and lock the door? I was beyond frightened, something told me it wouldn't make much of a difference what I tried to do. I would still be leaving with these two strangers tonight.

Rylan interrupted my internal debate, "Very good my son, you are stronger than you know. By your reaction earlier to us, I thought there was something special within you, now I know for sure." Rylan started to walk towards me, but I was completely rooted to the spot near the living room door. I wasn't sure what to think of what he had just said to me. I knew one thing for sure, strong and special were two words I wouldn't use to describe myself. He stopped right in front of me, I had to tilt my head completely back just to look at him.

"Get your things son. Bring only what you can carry. We can send someone later to gather the rest of your belongings." His voice sent a vibration through me that frightened me to my core. No way could I say no to this man, not when he stared at me with such intensity. Visions of being sacrificed, or worse, flashed through my mind, but my body betrayed me, and it did as he instructed.

I turned to walk up the stairs. As I hit the top step, I heard my mom behind me, offering to help me pack my things. I'm sure my dad was thrilled to be left behind with my biological parents, *or so they claimed.*

As soon as we turned into my room, my mom shut the door and looked at me. I had a feeling of déjà vu; not too long ago, my dad stood in exactly the same spot, for what I was sure a similar conversation.

"I love you, no matter what." She paused as she walked towards me, she grabbed and held my hands between us. "You can always come home, you can always call us. No matter what we are here for you, for the rest of our lives." She whispered.

I could tell she was doing all she could to hold herself together and keep her tears from streaming down her face. Unfortunately, I wasn't as strong, no matter what Rylan said, my tears ran down my cheeks. I didn't even have the strength to pull my hands from my mom's and wipe them away. I was still angry, furious, in fact. But that took second place to the reality that this was goodbye.

We pulled apart and stared at each other for a bit. Only then was I finally able to get something rational out, "Thank you mom, I love you and dad too, I'll visit I promise, I already miss you both." I choked out my words, but I was glad I got them out before I had to leave. I realized that I didn't have a choice. I'd be leaving my home soon with two people who have done nothing but intimidate me.

I mustered up the strength to remove my hands from my mom's and grab my stuff. I pocketed my dead cell phone that hadn't left my dresser in the last two days, as well as my wallet. I turn to grab my red backpack off my bed, but my mom had already grabbed it and walked to my door. I took one last look around, I had packed most of my stuff into boxes, and my fingers were crossed that I would be able to get them sent to me soon. I'd left a few belongings behind in hopes that I would be able to come home and visit soon, you know, *like tomorrow.*

I left my room and shut the door behind me. I took a deep breath and wiped my face roughly to get rid of the wetness. I needed to find as much courage as I could gather to walk down the stairs. I needed to be strong, just as Rylan suggested I was. I needed everything I could to get through this, I stood straight and looked square ahead as I headed back down to the living room. While I walked, I made a promise to myself. I promised I would make my mom and dad proud. They had given away the last eighteen years of their lives to take care of me, to love and support me. And no matter what biology said, they were my real parents and I wouldn't let them down!

When I made it to the bottom of the stairs I noticed everyone stood in silence as they waited for me, they looked uncomfortable. *Maybe my pep talk took longer than I thought.* I took my backpack from my mom and gave both my mom and dad a hug, I held each of them longer than I normally would have. I turned and looked at Rylan and Sila as they stood by the front door, it was clear they were in a hurry. I wasn't sure what to say, maybe there was nothing left to say. So I kept it simple as I turned back to my parents

"I'll call you when I get there." I thought about how I needed to charge my phone on the way. They both nodded and grinned through teary eyes.

I reached to open the door handle, turned it, pulled open the door and gestured for Rylan and Sila to walk out ahead of me. They nodded to my parents and walked out. I took what felt like my millionth deep breath in the last few days. I stole one last look at my parents and walked out the door into the night.

Chapter Three

Crickets were chirping outside as I shuffled out behind my new parents. The crickets didn't seem to care that the world as I knew it had come to an end. I followed behind Rylan and Sila to the driveway, which was on the side of the house, it was an old farmhouse that my dad and I had spent the better half of my life fixing up. It still needed quite a bit of work, but it was home nonetheless. I wasn't sure what kind of vehicle I expected to find in the driveway, but no vehicle was not something I had considered. *Did they take a taxi here? Maybe that means they lived close- except I knew pretty much everyone in this tiny country town.* Neither of them stopped when we arrived at the driveway. Without so much as a pause they continued to walk towards the road. *Where were they going?* They couldn't live that close. As we approached the end of the driveway, I stopped and looked both ways down the road in search of a car, but nope, nothing for as far as I could see.

I broke the silence, "Where are we going? No one has told me." I asked.

They both stopped to turn and look at me. "We're taking you home, and everyone is excited to meet you." Sila turned back around and continued to walk down the street.

We lived in the middle of nowhere, like literally in the middle of nowhere. The closest house was Eva's grandparents', and that was almost a mile away. *Did they really plan to just walk, in the pitch black dead of night, to wherever we were going? I thought.* "Umm, where exactly is home? Do you plan to walk there?" I started to have visions of being led to some remote location, where "their people" would tie me up and torture me or something. I began to wonder, again, who these two strangers were, and what propelled me to follow them into the night.

This time they both stopped and turned completely around to face me. They looked confused, like I should have known the answer to both of those questions. Rylan's voice boomed in the silent night as he answered, "We're taking you to Ochana, where you were born. I'm sure Michael and Ella have told you all about Ochana." Rylan stated. "Ahh, and of course we don't plan to walk, there's only one way to get there and it is way too far from here to walk." He shook his head at me and smirked, as if I had made a joke.

I was more confused now than before, my parents had never mentioned this place called Ochana, it didn't even sound familiar to me. I had no idea where it was, and if it was that far away, and we weren't going to walk, how were we getting there? I couldn't take it anymore, I needed them to answer my questions.

I planted my feet on the dirt road and refused to move. It took them a few seconds to realize I was no longer behind them. Rylan turned back around again and looked at me like I was a rebellious teenager. "What is it now? We are in a hurry," he huffed.

I gave him the best glare I could under the circumstances, as I stood in the dark, in the middle of nowhere, with two people I had no idea about and were bigger than any other person I had met before. Yea, I'm sure it looked more like a grimace than a glare, but I went with it. "I've never heard of Ochana, I have no idea where it is, and I have no idea how we are getting there. Now, can someone give me honest answers to my questions?" Because, let's face it I was starting to freak out again, but luckily I was smart enough to leave that part out.

Rylan and Sila looked from me then to each other, and an expression I couldn't decipher floated across their faces. "What exactly do you know?" Sila's voice had a cautious tone to it.

Dumbfounded, I just glared at her. I knew nothing; I felt like I was being kidnapped or something. Again, I was being stared at while they waited for an answer from me. *What did I know?* I began to summarize my understanding. "Well, you gave me up as a baby. My mom and dad adopted me, which I am still having a hard time grasping. They just told me this a few days ago. Oh and you guys are some kind of protectors and I am expected to be one as well." *What else was there?* The two of them had been so cryptic with me when I ask them questions. I was under the impression they weren't allowed to tell me anything, but here I was, stuck with two strangers who thought I knew everything that was going on.

Neither of them said a thing for a long while. I guess they wanted to choose their words with care. "We are protectors and you will be too." Rylan stated with confidence. "As for the rest, maybe we should show you. We were under the impression that Michael and Ella had already told you everything. Well, what they knew anyways." Rylan had tacked that last bit on a bit smug. "Now, I understand your confusion with how you reacted to our power," he added. Again, with the lack of answers, I guess they were worried about scaring me. Little did they know, I was way past scared.

Finding my courage, I told them, "Then show me. No more of these meaningless answers." I hoped that was the right thing to say, no more secrets. It's what I've wanted all along.

Rylan looked around, I wasn't sure what he was looking for, not like anything was around, being the middle of nowhere and all. We were surrounded by trees, I could still see the lights from my house, *my parents' house.* The sky was clear, except for a few stars that were out, the moon hung high, casting an eerie glow onto the ground. Rylan took off towards the tree line, Sila stayed quiet next to me, but did not follow. I wasn't sure if I was supposed to stay with her or follow Rylan into the trees. Curiosity won and I headed towards Rylan, but Sila stopped me with a hand on my shoulder. This was the first real contact I had with either Rylan or Sila. Her touch sent a shiver through my body.

"Stay here, open your senses and stay calm."

Stay calm? Was a pack of werewolves or something going to fly out of the woods? I almost asked her as much, but held my tongue at the last minute, not wanting her to see that side of me. I could no longer see Rylan, *what was he doing?*

Finally, I heard a rustling, like someone, I assume Rylan was coming towards us from the trees. I squinted towards them, but saw nothing. Sila looked down at me with a face of comfort and ease. She waited for me to see. See what, I wasn't sure.

Finally giving up, I looked at Sila and asked, "Where did Rylan go?" I paused after my question, I realized that I had called Rylan by his name and not father, or dad, or whatever I was supposed to call him. No introductions were officially made yet.

Sila said nothing, but gestured with her hands for me to continue looking at the trees. What was it she had said to me? *Open my senses?* I concentrated on opening my senses, nothing seemed to be happening though. I turned back to Sila and she again gestured towards the trees. I growled in frustration. I looked back at the trees, squinting once again.

Sila's voice echoed around me almost melodically, "Relax. Feel it, deep within you. I promise, my son, it's there inside of you."

I closed my eyes and took my millionth and one deep breath, then relaxed. I opened my eyes and looked out towards the trees. I felt different, more in touch, with what I wasn't sure yet. I could also feel something within me, something I had never felt before, something no words could describe. I felt whole, like I had been missing something and never knew.

I continued to relax as I stood next to Sila in the dark, with nothing but the moon and a few stray stars for light. Out of nowhere, I saw something. It blended with the trees, like camouflage. It looked to be some kind of animal, but much larger than any animal I had ever seen. My eyes were playing games on me, what I thought I saw couldn't exist. Didn't exist, it was impossible. I started to shake, forgetting to relax and stay calm. It seemed Sila must have seen I was about to lose it.

"My son, it is alright. What you see is real, he would never hurt you. That my son, is your father." She grabbed my shoulders, in what seemed to be an attempt to stop my shaking.

I knew it was Rylan the second my eyes landed on him. Somehow I knew, I felt it, but that didn't take the fear away. If anything, it amplified it. If that thing was my father, then what was I? My eyes stayed on Rylan, "What is he?" I whispered, not wanting to startle Rylan.

I could feel Sila as she looked at me, I somehow sensed her *energy* towards me. "I think you know, my son. I need you to answer that question. Dig deep within you and do not be afraid. What is it you see?"

Of course she couldn't just answer my question, why make anything easy for me. I blew out the breath I had been holding in and answered her hesitantly, "He...he is a dragon?" I questioned. Thinking it in my head and saying it out loud were two completely different things. Saying it out loud made it that much realer.

Sila squeezed my shoulders, I hadn't realized she still held me, "You are correct. No need to question what your eyes see." She let go of my shoulders and stepped to the side of me. She continued, "Your father, as am I, are green dragons, or Leslos as we call them in Ochana. We were born of fire and made with Earth, Leslos are the leaders of Ochana." Sila turned towards Rylan.

Unbelievable. My parents were dragons. I continued to stare at Rylan, the dragon, I wouldn't have believed it if I hadn't seen it with my own eyes. I guess that's what he'd meant by it being best to show me, there was no way I would have believed them otherwise. I hesitated a second as I attempted to get my thoughts straight. Questions raced through my head, I wasn't sure where to start. I finally broke my eyes away from Rylan and turned to Sila.

"Why couldn't I see him at first? Now that I see him, I don't see how anyone could miss him." He was gigantic, like a tyrannosaurs rex. He almost reached the tops of the old pine trees.

Sila ignored my question, "We need to leave, the only way we are going to make it back to Ochana tonight is if we hurry," she walked towards Rylan.

I still didn't know where Ochana was or how we planned on getting there. It seemed my questions were endless as of late, and wholly unanswered. I started to follow Sila across the road towards the trees where Rylan still stood as a Leslo, as Sila had called him. The closer we made it to Rylan, the more my eyes were able to pick up the details of the magnificent creature in front of me. It was like nothing I had ever seen before. Rylan was brilliant, a spectrum of glistening green hues radiated the sky dust around his figure, and even though the darkness made it almost impossible to see the exact shade of green he was, I could tell it was miraculous.

A thought popped into my head and before I could stop myself I blurted it out, "Wait, if you both are dragons, then what am I?" I halted in the middle of the road. Luckily this part of Clover was deserted, with just a few houses, miles between each other. The thought disturbed me for some reason. I mean if my parents were dragons, wouldn't that make me one?

Sila paused ahead of me and turned slowly until she faced me. I could see the wheels as they turned in her head as she thought about her next words carefully. "My son, you are more than just a dragon." She paused to read my expression on my face, then continued, "You are the son of two very powerful Leslos and our expectations for you are high. We have expectations for who and what you'll be."

After that last bit, she smiled like I should be happy about her declaration. I began to wonder if they had even picked up the right kid. I mean, I was just ordinary Cole. I was never good at anything, just a normal kid. As stated, Rylan and Sila had expectations for me, unrealistic ones at that. This scared me more than the dragon standing less than twenty feet away.

Chapter Four

We caught up to Rylan a few moments later. I was still confused as to what the plan was to get to Ochana without a mode of transportation. Sila and Rylan didn't seem concerned at all. I watched as Sila walked behind Rylan. I began to follow, but got a huff from Rylan, which I assumed meant to stay put. Sila had left me alone with a massive green dragon, something that shouldn't exist, that also happened to be my father. My mind raced over everything I had learned in the last five minutes. My mind covered every possible option of who my parents were and what they would be like the last two days, but I never even came close to reality.

Suddenly, another disconcerted presence jolted me from my internal thoughts. I looked up to see another green dragon, or Leslo that stood next to Rylan. Well, at least I knew where Sila had gone.

They both gazed at me, waiting for something. I knew they couldn't answer me, but I asked anyways, "Now what? How are we getting to Ochana?" I waited a few seconds for a response. Nothing. Not that I had expected one. I looked around, for what I didn't know. All I saw were trees and a vacant road. I looked back up at Rylan and Sila, I waited in silence for some kind of signal as to what to do next.

Then, that lyrical voice from Sila echoed in my head, literally in my head. "Son, you'll ride on your father's back. There's no other way to get to Ochana, but to fly. Unless, you're able to shift into your dragon?"

Startled, I tried to process the fact that Sila's voice was inside my head, then I thought about what she said. I had no idea how to turn myself into a dragon, I didn't even know where to start. I walked as close to Rylan as I could. He bent down so I could climb onto his scaly back. The feeling was awkward, there wasn't a saddle or harness. I positioned myself between two *spikes*, I'm sure there was a technical name for them, but I didn't know it. I wrapped my arms around the one in front of me and sent a prayer up to my guardian angel that I wouldn't fall. Rylan's skin felt rugged and dry, not slimy like I had expected.

Rylan walked out into the middle of the road and spread his wings out. He was even bigger than I had first thought; his wings touched the trees on each side of the road. There was no way this wasn't going to end without me falling to my death.

I tightened my hold around Rylan. My arms shook with the strength I was using to hold on and we hadn't even left the ground yet. I heard a snort behind us and turned around in time to see Sila step behind Rylan and spread out her wings, just as Rylan had. The sight amazed me.

Rylan took my distraction of Sila as an opportunity to scare the heck out of me. He hastily crouched his legs and hurled me into his front spike. I refastened my hands around it just in time as he pushed off the ground and climbed into the sky. I squeezed my eyes shut and sucked in a breath, I'd never been more terrified then I was at that moment. I hoped my ride on the back of a dragon would be a short one.

We ascended into the sky for just a few minutes, then leveled off. I took a large breath and cracked open my eyes. I was shocked by the site that surrounded me; a dark sky with just the moon as our guide. I relaxed a bit around Rylan and started to look around more with ease. I had never been in an airplane, so seeing the ground from the air was all new to me. I could see the lights from the ground looking up at me just as the stars had looked down at me so many nights before.

The excitement began to wean and I felt exhausted. My adrenaline had worn off as the whole night finally caught up to me. The last thing I needed was to fall asleep and plummet to my death. I still had a lot of questions, seeing as Sila was able to answer me before in her Leslo form, I went for it. "Sila, how long until we arrive in Ochana?" My question was met with silence for a few minutes, maybe she couldn't hear me. I thought animals had better hearing then humans, but I didn't know anything about dragon hearing.

"We will arrive in about two hours son. You'll find that our time is remarkably fast considering the distance we will be traveling."

Two hours? It would be a struggle to keep my eyes open, but it was better than the alternative. It would give me the time to think through everything, maybe Sila would be open to answering some more of my questions since all we seemed to have was time.

"Where is Ochana located?" It was a question I had had for the last two days, not about Ochana, but about where my new home would be.

It took Sila a few minutes again to answer, "Ochana is high above the clouds, off the coast of Greenland."

Wow, we planned to fly all the way to Greenland? Sila stated it would only take a few hours, I could only imagine the speed we were traveling at for that to be true. It felt like we were merely floating, not speeding through the air. My mind raced as to what it must be like there. My knowledge of Greenland was limited. I knew it was cold, like really cold but that was it. That thought made me wonder about my present situation. I should be cold now, but I wasn't, if anything, I was warm.

Sila interrupted my thoughts, "Very good son, your thoughts are loud and clear. You aren't cold because I don't will you to be. You will learn about this will. We call it mahier. Mahier is an old Ochana word, it is what makes us dragons. You will learn later what that entails."

Sila's unexpected disruption only gave me more questions. She could read my thoughts? I'm sure she has gotten a real laugh out of all my inward jibber jabber since we met. I hoped I hadn't completely embarrassed myself. Mahier, eh? It would take some time to be able to say it like Sila had, with her harmonious voice, but I wondered about it. Was it like magic? A few hours ago, something like magic would be laughable to me, but now anything was possible.

Since she was willing me to be warm, was she willing me to feel like we were floating as well? I wondered what else she was capable of. I had almost forgotten about Rylan, he didn't seem to be able to talk to me while as a Leslo like Sila, or he didn't want to talk to me, which could be a real possibility too.

I looked around at my new surroundings, we must have traveled quite far by now. Time was a concept I had no clue of while flying on the back of a dragon, and there was no way I was letting go of Rylan to check my watch. As I looked around, I noticed what looked like snow on the ground. I had seen little snow in my time in Texas, though I had always wanted to try snowmobiling or skiing, maybe with my new life, I finally could?

The ground grew closer, and Rylan had begun to descend. It astounded me how I could barely feel any of this. It looked like we were going to land in an empty field. Everywhere I looked, all I could see was snow. *Surely this wasn't Ochana?*

Rylan's clawed feet hit the ground with a quiet thud. I squeezed him tighter, afraid I would fall off from the impact. Thankfully I was able to hold on and stay put. Rylan leaned down as a signal for me to climb off. I leapt off and turned towards Sila, who had already transformed back into her human form. She really was stunning, it was hard to believe she was my mother. I was relieved to see she transformed back with clothes on, it must be part of the mahier she talked about earlier. She turned to me and beamed a knowing smile my way.

"How do you feel? Your first flight seemed successful." She winked at me and gave a slight chuckle.

Well, I didn't fall so I would call that a success. "I'm starting to feel tired, are we there?" I looked every which way to see something that would tell me where we were, but there was nothing except sheets of snow everywhere I looked.

Rylan stepped towards me. He was back in his human form, also clothed. "We're close," Rylan assured. "This is Ellesmere Island, Canada. We're resting for a bit, we have traveled quite a distance."

Geography was something I never paid much attention to, and all I knew about Canada was that it was in the North. I regretted not paying more attention in school.

"However, we need to get you in touch with your dragon in order to continue our trip and enter Ochana."

I should've guessed it wouldn't be as easy as just hitching a ride on the back of a dragon. How was I supposed to get in touch with my dragon? I didn't even know if there really was a dragon to get in touch with. I looked at Rylan and Sila with an expression that I hoped showed my true distress on this matter.

Rylan chuckled, "Relax son, you've already proven your strength to us. You're able to control our mahier. It's how you were able to take control back of your being after your mother ordered you to leave at the house." Rylan nodded toward Sila as he said 'mother.' He continued, "Only a very strong dragon, especially one with no experience, could accomplish that."

Rylan's revelation didn't make me feel any better. I wasn't thinking about dragons and mahier, or much of anything back at the house. My only concern then was not wanting to leave. How would I explain to Rylan that I wasn't as strong as he thought I was, that it was just a mistake? Something I never had control over.

Sila grabbed my shoulders, much like she did when I first saw Rylan as a Leslo. Her green eyes pierced into my brown, "But you are strong son, I can feel it. When we landed at your house tonight, your father and I were both in our Leslo forms, it is why your body reacted the way it did. You haven't been in the presence of such power since you were a baby. Your body was recalling that power, the mahier. You will find your dragon. I can promise you that." Sila dropped her arms from me and walked towards Rylan.

He had walked about two hundred yards from us to set up some kind of makeshift camp. Where did he find all those supplies? Sila angled herself towards me and mouthed the word "mahier." I would have to remember that Sila could read my thoughts. It was definitely something I would have to get used to.

As I got closer to Rylan, I noticed he had set up two tents and started a fire, and was already cooking something over it. I was impressed, he had set up camp in the middle of a frozen desert. I hoped they were right about me, I'd love to be able to do the things they were able to. I took a seat next to Sila in a chair that seemed to appear from thin air, I peered over the fire as Rylan cooked.

"Where do I start? I mean, with finding my dragon, how do I do that?" I wasn't asking either of them in particular, I just hoped one of them would answer.

"It's different for everyone. Everyone has a unique relationship with their dragon. It also depends on your type of dragon. Rylan and I are Leslos, but there are other types. Each type has its own responsibilities and purpose." Sila took a breath and looked at me, "Just concentrate son. Reach out towards your dragon. Let him know you're ready to accept him. He will appear, in one form or another."

Concentrate on my dragon. It seemed much easier than it was. Once I found my dragon, would I just shift into it? I'll be honest, I was terrified, and I bet it hurt a whole lot to shift. I wondered what it would feel like, would we be separate or become one? I was so confused, my focus was not on finding my dragon, my mind was scattered in thoughts.

Rylan waved a plate of food in front of me. I wasn't sure exactly what it was, some sort of meat that smelled delicious. I grabbed the plate from him. Rylan sat back down and started to eat, I stared at him in wonder. He had already scarfed down more food than I eat in a whole day, and he didn't seem to be slowing down. If he always ate this way, I had no idea how he was in such good shape.

A chuckle came from beside me, "It takes a lot to shift son, and your father is not only feeding himself, but his dragon. Usually we would feed while in our Leslo forms, but we didn't have the time tonight to do so. Now eat, you will need your strength, then we will leave you alone to connect with your dragon. Your father will need about an hour to rest and gain all his mahier back."

That was interesting, Rylan lost some of his mahier and needed to rest, yet Sila seemed just fine. Maybe Sila was stronger than Rylan, by looking at the two of them I thought for sure Rylan was stronger.

"Your father had to use his mahier more than I did. Rylan protected us as we flew, no human was able to detect us. My job was much simpler, all I had to do was protect you." Sila pointed at me with that last bit.

It all made sense now, I had felt like we floated here, when in reality we had sped through the sky. It also answered my question as to why Rylan didn't speak as we flew, he was focused elsewhere. At least some things started to make sense. Now I just needed to find my dragon.

I finished eating and watched as Rylan stepped into one of the tents. Sila took my plate and placed it on top of hers and set them by the fire. She nodded at me and stepped into the same tent as Rylan. I sat there alone. Finally, just one thought was in my head, how to find my dragon.

Chapter Five

Finding my dragon wasn't going to be easy. I mean, if I had a dragon, wouldn't I have already found it in the last eighteen years? Taking a deep breath, I closed my eyes and pictured what I wanted my dragon to look like. The dragon I pictured was strong and powerful, a Leslo like Rylan and Sila. It stood taller than both of them, its wing spanned at least twice theirs.

I concentrated hard on the image in my mind. Nothing happened. I opened my eyes and kicked at the sticks by my feet that Rylan had left for the fire. I felt nothing, my first request by my biological parents had to be to turn into a dragon, and I felt like I was about to fail them.

I thought about my mom and dad and how they would've reacted to my situation. It was obvious to me now that they knew what I was or what I was to become. Even with that knowledge, they loved and supported me. They were always proud of me, no matter what little I actually succeeded in. I remembered my promise I made to myself before I left home. I wasn't going to let them down! With this new encouragement, I took yet another breath and tried again.

This time I didn't picture what my dragon would look like, as I remembered what Sila had said about different types of dragons. Instead, I thought about the traits I would want my dragon to have. Strong, fair, kind and smart. These traits made me think of my friend Eva. Apparently, I wanted my dragon to be like her. I shook my head and cleared my mind of my friend. I again focused on my dragon.

My breath evened out, almost like I was asleep. Everything around me faded away. It was just me. There, deep within, I felt it. Almost like I was being pulled towards something. I concentrated on it. I tried to grab onto the pull I felt and reel it in.

My breath caught in my throat, something was happening. I was no longer in control, my body started to shake, my vision blurred around the edges. I looked down at my hands in time to see my fingers turn into claws, they were ginormous and sharp. My body pitched forward until I was laid out on the ground on my stomach. I tried to stand back up but I had no control of my arms. I watched as shimmering scales burst through my skin of my hands and feet. My scales progressed until they covered my whole body. I looked behind me in time to see spikes as they emerged out of my spine, a tail covered in thorns grew out of the bottom of my back, like it had sprouted from my tailbone. I gasped as the wind was taken from me, on either side of the spikes gigantic wings ripped through me. My head started to expand and I could feel two horns pierce through each side of my head.

Then everything stopped. I tried to take inventory of my new form, but my movements were awkward. I no longer had complete control of myself. I stood on all fours, right where our makeshift camp used to be. Even though I knew what had just happened, and had even asked for it, I was terrified.

"Breathe son, your dragon is in control, and you mustn't be afraid. Reach out to your dragon, become one."

For the first time I was thankful Sila could read my mind. I did as she had said, I began to breathe slower while I tried to reach out to my dragon. I focused my thoughts, I felt a twinge resounded in the back of my mind. It felt like I was being connected to something or joined. A feeling of peace surrounded me.

Rylan's voice startled me, "Very good son, your transformation was quicker than I had expected. Many dragons in the past had been stuck right where you stand for months as they waited for their dragons to appear."

Months? I was frustrated with the few minutes I couldn't find mine. I was unable to imagine the toll a wait that long would cost someone. The thought alone made me shiver.

"That thought son is what will make you special amongst our race. Empathy is not a feeling many Ochana's possess." She paused to examine me, "Your color is one I haven't seen before." A curious look was exchanged between Sila and Rylan.

Until that comment I had felt confident in my new dragon state. A color they hadn't seen before? What did that mean? I had hoped to just blend in when we arrived at Ochana.

"Our council will be able to explain your color, I'm sure it's a sign of strength. For you, son, will be strong." I had waited for Rylan to smile about this, but instead he gave a little nod and walked away.

I watched intently as Rylan shifted into his dragon, it was much smoother than mine had been, which was difficult and chaotic for me, though now that I thought about it, painless. Rylan was so sure I would be strong, I hoped I didn't disappoint him.

Sila walked over to me and placed her hand on my shoulder, well my dragon shoulder. "You could not disappoint your father in any way. You have no idea how proud he is of you." She turned to approach Rylan and shifted as she walked toward him. Her shift was even more fluid than Rylan's. If I had blinked, I would've missed it.

I stood behind them as I waited to see what to do next, they hadn't told me anything. I could barely walk as a dragon, I couldn't even imagine trying to fly. I looked over towards them as we walked, they were so much larger than me. I wondered, was it because of my age or the type of dragon I was?

"Do not worry, you will grow." Sila angled her head towards me as her voice flowed through me. "It is time to learn to fly."

Rylan kicked off the ground and flew into the sky. The sight amazed me. A powerful green dragon circled us from above. I watched how his body moved, I tried to memorize his movements. He continued to circle us as he moved further up into the sky, until he looked like nothing more than a bird flying above us.

"Your turn."

I was so engrossed in watching Rylan, Sila's voice startled me. My turn? I had no idea how to start, Rylan had just kicked off the ground and took off. He made it look simple.

"There's your answer son. Once you get up, your dragon instincts will take over." Sila gestured for me to get on with it.

What's the worst that could happen? *Falling, crashing....dying.* I tried not to think of the real possibility of this ending horribly, so instead I shifted my focus on moving my dragon body the way I needed it to. I walked a few feet away from Sila, but I found the simple task of walking difficult, which didn't leave me confident with flying. I squatted down as low as I could, I dug my clawed feet into the snow, pushed myself off the ground with all my might and spread my wings. I made it about twenty feet from the ground before I fell back down to the earth. I hit the snow with a loud thud and my whole body shuddered. I shook the snow off and turned toward Sila for guidance.

With a quiet chuckle, Sila's smooth voice filtered through my dazed brain. "Do not fret son, I have never met a dragon who flew on their first try. It may take some time. Once you're up, stay there and follow Rylan and I, we will guide you to Ochana." With that, Sila took off towards Rylan, and they both circled me from above.

They hovered in the air with their eyes focused on me. Rylan seemed to be in such a hurry all night to get back to Ochana. I needed to get myself together and up into the air. I was so worried about Rylan being disappointed in me, he was so sure I was going to be this super strong dragon. I wanted to be that for him, I didn't understand my need to make him proud. I dodged that thought and tried to clear my mind, except for one thought, fly.

I shook the snow off once again, leaned down until my chest almost touched the ground, pulled my wings back and kicked as hard as I could off the ground. Once I was about thirty feet up I took a deep breath and spread my wings out. I started to glide, the feeling was incredible. Then I started to descend down to the ground, I needed to fly not glide. I moved my wings up and down. My dragon instincts began to take over as I flew higher and higher. My movements were choppy and clumsy, but it was enough to get me close to Rylan and Sila.

Rylan took off towards the clouds while Sila stayed back with me as we followed behind him at a much slower pace. I started to fly without thought, it felt like my body just knew what to do. With this new freedom, I could focus my attention on my surroundings. It was still night, but the moon and stars seemed brighter than before. I could see the clouds as we weaved through them. The sight took my breath away. I thought I would have been scared, being so far off the ground. Instead, I felt unafraid, almost fearless, like nothing bad could happen to me. At least not in my dragon form.

I couldn't see Rylan anymore, so I stayed close to Sila, she didn't seem to pay any mind to me as she flew. Everything that happened in the last few hours still left me stunned. How could this possibly be my life? A dragon. Imagine that? I couldn't, not in my wildest dreams did I ever think dragons existed, or that I would be one. Sila veered right and I followed her. We flew over water. It was beautiful, frozen patches covered the majority of it.

"This is the Lincoln Sea, it is part of the Arctic Ocean. Human population in this area is near extinction, it is why this location was chosen for Ochana. We are free to come and go undetected with ease. The water here is frozen quite thick, so the vibrations from our wings go unnoticed, with the support of our mahier."

That knowledge ignited many questions about my future home; however, I wasn't sure how to communicate with Sila as a dragon to ask. I hadn't heard Rylan speak as a dragon, so I figured it wasn't a skill all had.

Sila's laugh pulsed through my head, "Son, I hear you loud and clear, through your thoughts. It is how I am communicating with you. I am projecting my thoughts. Your father can do this as well, but his focus is elsewhere. Your father has already made contact with Ochana, the council will be ready to receive you when we arrive."

Council, I wondered about them. Who were they? Would they have answers about my color? Were they the dragons in charge? I focused on Sila, "How long until we arrive?" I hoped I was able to project like she had explained.

"We're almost there. Don't be nervous. The council is very excited to meet you. They have been waiting for eighteen years for you. It may seem like an insignificant amount of time in a dragon's life, but we have waited for you for much longer than your short life thus far."

Before I had a chance to comprehend what Sila had just told me, she darted upwards. The angle was difficult to follow, right when I thought for sure I couldn't continue, Sila leveled out and began to descend. I looked out in front of her and noticed what looked like an island, only instead of being surrounded by water, it was surrounded by clouds. A large waterfall fell freely off the side, disappearing into the clouds. I watched as Rylan landed effortlessly next to the magnificent waterfall.

Sila landed smoothly onto the island, which I believed to be Ochana. I braced myself for my first landing, I hit the ground rough, and stumbled forward hard with a crash. I picked myself up in time to find Rylan and Sila as they observed me in their human forms. Behind them were four individuals who looked to be just a few years older than my parents. I inspected the others as thoroughly as they inspected me. They each had a very distinctive trait that separated them. The characteristic that stuck out most were their eyes, each a different color; but still, like Rylan and Sila, they stood out like gems.

This must be the council.

Chapter Six

We all stared at each other for some time, my nervousness was beginning to show as my hands trembled. I couldn't get a good read on the council, they showed no emotion, but their eyes never left me. I wondered what they thought about me as they studied me. This would be a great time to know how to read minds like Sila. I need her to teach me that next.

Rylan broke the silence as he commanded the attention of the council, "It is my honor to introduce my son, Colton, Prince of Ochana."

I looked at Rylan after he finished. *Prince?* I must have heard wrong. No one had said anything to me about being a Prince or royalty. This can't be right, I'm just Cole, not Colton, not Prince. I can't be a Prince.

A woman with long black hair bowed to me in respect before she spoke, "King Rylan, Queen Sila, we are glad to see you have returned so quickly. Your stay at Ellesmere Island must have been a short one. That is a very good sign of things to come." Finally she broke her stare from me, and her bright blue eyes looked towards Rylan.

"Jules, you will find that my son is quite remarkable, as you can see even his color is unique." Rylan gestured towards me then turned towards the other councilmen. "Let's take this conversation inside, we have much to discuss now that the Prince has returned." Rylan turned and walked about a hundred feet, he stopped beside the waterfall, with a wave of his hands the water ceased. He continued to walk, until I could no longer see him.

The council followed behind him. One councilmen, the one with calculating red eyes shot me a look over his shoulder before he disappeared with the rest. Sila came over to me, and placed her hand on my shoulder. I could tell she was trying to relax my fear. She had a calmness to her that in return cleared a bit of my anxiety.

"I need you to change back to your human form, the council will want to speak with you." She informed me.

Her voice calmed my nerves a bit more as she spoke, until I registered what she said, "How do I change?" I hoped she could hear me.

"Just as you found your dragon, you now need to find your human."

I pictured myself as I knew me to be. My mop of brown hair that constantly fell in my face, my dull brown eyes, lanky limbs and thin physique. I felt a now familiar twinge in the back of my head. I grabbed on to this feeling, like I did with my dragon and started to change. My body jerked for long moments, until I found myself sitting on the ground by Sila's feet. I looked up and found a smile had formed on her face as she looked down at me. She reached her hand down to help me up, I grabbed on and lifted myself off the ground. Once up, she continued to hold my hand as we walked through the waterfall. Once through, Sila looked back towards the entrance and the water began to fall once more.

We walked through a series of caves. On the walls there were pictures painted and words I didn't understand. The pictures showed dragons and humans alike throughout history. They were hard to decipher without knowing the history behind them but I could see that humans and dragons had been connected since the beginning of time, based on the evolution of man in the drawings. I couldn't wait to take a closer look, whoever painted them was very talented, and I was amazed by the drawings.

Sila squeezed my hand, "Soon you will learn all about our history and relationship with the humans. Some of it will be hard to hear and will anger you. Keep an open mind as you listen." She looked over at me as she spoke, "First, we need to get your training schedule prepared. Then, I will show you around Ochana and our home."

We finally arrived into a large square room. The first thing I noticed was that the room didn't have a ceiling. When I looked up the evening sky looked down on me. My eyes shifted to the four walls, each wall displayed a picture of a different colored dragon. The first wall showed a huge red dragon with fire shooting out of its mouth while it appeared to be in combat against a black, shadowy figure. The word "Woland" was carved into the wall towards the bottom. The second wall exhibited a blue dragon who stood next to what appeared to be a large bird's nest full of eggs. The word "Galian" was carved into the wall alongside the image. I decided to wander to the third wall, and saw a silver dragon who pulled a cart of fruits and vegetables behind it. The word "Sien" was etched on the wall below the image. Finally, the last wall showed a dragon I was familiar with, a large green dragon who stood at the top of a cliff, its head raised high. The word "Leslo" was written on it. I took another quick look at each picture, I figured these must be the different types of dragons, and the images depict the jobs and responsibilities of each dragon.

I turned away from the last image to face my parents and the council, they had all taken seats around the huge round table placed in the middle of the room. Rylan and Sila sat next to each other, but I noticed there were two empty chairs next to Sila, and three next to Rylan, while the council occupied the remainder of the seats. Sila commanded I have a seat as she pointed to the spot next to Rylan. As I sat, I gazed at the empty seats and wondered who would fill them.

"Son, I would like to introduce you to your council. The Keepers, as they are known by, is formed of elders who represent the four founding dragons. As I'm sure you have noticed, dragons are distinguished by their color. Your mother and I are green dragons, or Leslos, as is Allas." Rylan gestured towards an African American woman with shining green eyes. "We are the leaders of Ochana, our family has been in command for many generation. You will find that Leslos are the rarest dragon and the only dragon equipped to lead."

"Prince, it is an honor to see you again." Allas bowed her head slightly towards me. *Again?* I don't remember meeting her.

"Blue dragons, or Galians, are our guardians and nurturers." Rylan pointed at a woman with brilliant blue eyes and black hair, "You met Jules when we first arrived."

"I will guide you in any way you need, Prince," Jules then bowed to me too.

"Seins, or silver dragons are our workers, they keep Ochana running in all day to day operations." Gesturing towards a man with gray eyes and a strong exterior, "Luka is a Sein."

"My Prince," Luka bowed deeply to me.

"And lastly, red dragons, or Wolands, are warriors who protect everything you see. Jericho is one of the strongest of these warriors."

The last unknown occupant at the table glared at me, he said nothing. He made me nervous, his eyes almost glowed red, and his dark hair concealed most of his face. His eyes tracked each of my movements. Silently, he filed away his observations.

Rylan ignored Jericho's reaction towards me, I hoped this was his usual disposition with others, not just me. I broke eye contact with him and glanced around the table at the rest of the council. Rylan stated these were the elders, which was odd, the oldest of the elders appeared to only be in their late thirties. The four councilmen regarded Rylan, as they waited for his next directive.

"As you all have noticed, the Prince has a matchless color of our four founding dragons. The Prince is strong, stronger than any newly hatched dragon I've met. Do any of you have an explanation for this?" Rylan searched the faces of each councilman as he spoke.

I observed the reaction each member of the council had with Rylan's question. Each reacted differently. Jericho continued to glare at me unbothered by the question as the other three looked towards each other with a look of bewilderment. Jules seemed the most on edge by the question, I was surprised she was the first to answer.

"Your Highness." Jules looked towards Rylan with a fearful expression on her face. "We have seen rare dragon appearances before, many times." She paused and looked around the table, as if she was hoping someone else would finish her thought, or at least support its significance. "The dramon's, my King, they never fit just one Ochana." Her eyes dropped to the table when she finished.

"Jules, don't be absurd! You are talking about the Prince of Ochana, no way could he be a dramon. That thought can never leave this table. The backlash would destroy Ochana." Luka looked furious at Jules as he refuted her idea.

The room went silent for a minute as everyone reflected on what was just discussed. What was a dramon? Was I some kind of mutant? I looked over at Sila and caught her as she assessed me. She nodded her head at me with encouragement, a small smile on her lips. She wanted me to ask my question out loud.

I coughed into my hand to clear my throat. Every eye in the room focused on me. "Umm, what's a dramon?" My voiced cracked as I spoke, I had hoped to sound certain of myself. That wasn't happening.

"Son, a dramon is a half-human, half-dragon. They are rarer than Leslos. You need not worry son, you would not be at this table if you were one. Only true blooded dragons are able to enter Ochana." Rylan shifted his body and glared at Jules, his body shook as his voice reverberated. "You accuse our Queen of treason with the accusation of Prince Colton's parentage?" His question carried the promise of a threat.

The statement lingered in the air before Jules responded, her voice shook in distress. "King Rylan, Queen Sila, my intention was never to question the Prince's parentage. I was only-"

Rylan cut her off with a wave of his hands and a look that froze her to her seat, "I am the King of Ochana. Prince Colton is my son. Do not ever question my claim again." Rylan released Jules from his hold and turned towards Sila. "My Queen, accept my apology, I am confident my council never questioned your faithfulness."

Sila seemed unbothered by the accusation, she placed her calming hand on Rylan's, "My King, Jules has a responsibility to all of Ochana, and it is her due diligence to explore all possible reasons for the Prince's color. Jules is right. A dramon's color does not fit into one of our four."

"My King," Allas bowed her head as she waited for permission to continue. "When the Prince arrived, I closely observed his unique color. The remarkable hues do in fact fit into our four founders. If my recollections are correct, each of the Prince's scales show of one distinct color, but each scale was different from the next.

"What do you mean Allas?" Rylan gave her a look of impatience.

"My King, each one of Prince Colton's scales were one of four colors. Red, green, blue and silver." Allas seemed unsure as she looked to each councilmen for assurance. "Woland, Leslo, Galian and Sein." She explained.

The long silence broke with Rylan's enthusiasm, "Amazing, you truly are remarkable son, as I knew you would be!" Rylan answered with a proud look, he pounded his fist on the table as he persisted. "Jericho, I expect you to personally train the Prince in combat." He looked to Jericho for his confirmation.

Rylan left no room for an objection. I looked towards Jericho after Rylan's declaration. He continued to show no emotion as he nodded once in his agreement. I still hadn't heard a peep from the man's mouth. Rylan continued to give orders to his council. Each member would be responsible to train me in one way or another. His last order was to meet again in the morning, each member would be held responsible to conduct historical research on dragons who resembled me. He wanted to have an in depth conversation about it.

The council showed respect to their King and Queen once more before they left for the night.

Rylan and Sila faced me. Rylan still seemed elated with the news of my color. I didn't understand his delight, we had no real answers as to what my color meant.

"You must have many questions, son. Let's go for a walk. We can talk as we show you your new home. The people of Ochana are excited with your return." Sila walked towards the cave we had entered from earlier.

Rylan waved his hands in gesture for Sila and me to follow ahead of him. As I passed by, he grabbed my arm, "Prepare yourself son." With that, he let go of my arm and waited for me to walk behind Sila.

Once back in the cave, Rylan began to explain some of the images that passed by us on the walls. Most of the pictures depicted historical milestones for Ochana. Rylan stopped in front of one, he waited for me to turn and give him my full attention.

"I have waited for you to ask." He paused, "Do you not wonder why you were not raised here on Ochana?"

I absorbed the painting's contents he stopped in front of. A green dragon, or Leslo, had a large speckled egg held tight within its claws. A human woman stood in front of the dragon with her hands held out towards the egg.

"Dragons are protectors. We protect all that is true. However, there was a time in our history when we forgot our purpose. We hid away on Ochana from all that surrounded us." He looked towards another painting on the opposite wall.

For the first time he looked anxious, even apprehensive. The painting was much different than the others. In all the other images the dragons were strong, clear winners in whatever was going on at that time. However, in this particular drawing, a large black-hooded figure hovered over humans, who cowered in its presence. The humans looked scared, many of them crying. A large fire was in the background. I realized there weren't any dragons in this picture.

"A powerful Woland named Jago came to our council one night. He was fatigued and panicked. He had just finished his checks around Ochana." Rylan paused, taking a deep breath. "He was halfway back to his command center when his mahier started to wane. He went straight to our council, where Jago explained what had happened. He had just finished his explanation when he fainted. Our healers rushed to his side, but they were unable to stabilize him; his mahier had completely diminished. Without mahier, a dragon is unable to survive on Ochana."

Rylan looked at the ground, his shoulders shook, almost like he had just relived the whole experience firsthand. I had never seen Rylan like this. The Rylan I knew was strong and powerful, the man who stood in front of me now was not.

Rylan looked up and placed both of his hands on my shoulders. "Jago was my eldest brother. He was one of the strongest, most powerful Wolands ever. We were reminded that day of our purpose. We had neglected our responsibilities as protectors, and as punishment our strongest warrior perished." Rylan dropped his hands from my shoulders and turned towards the image on the wall. "Our council decided soon after that, we needed a constant reminder of what we protect and why. It was proclaimed, all dragon infants would be handed over to humans until their eighteenth birthday."

Sila grabbed my hand to catch my attention, "The relationships you formed with the family who raised you and the friends who stood by you, will stay with you for always. Keep those memories close, because your future as a protector will not be an easy one."

Sila took Rylan's hand and began to walk towards the waterfall that would lead us to the rest of Ochana. I stood and stared at the black hooded figure in the painting, I wondered just what my life would entail here on Ochana. I wanted nothing more than to be faced with my black-holed life. I wished my mother was here- I didn't know these people, they weren't my family. I knew I was about to cry. I closed my eyes and took a breath.

Chapter Seven

I jolted awake from my slumber. A feeling of uncertainty overwhelmed me. I had one of the most vivid dreams of my life. As I lifted myself up and absorbed my surroundings, I realized it wasn't a dream at all. The more awoke I became, the clearer the night before came back to me. Rylan, Sila and I had decided to just head to bed after story time. I didn't take in much of my new home as we headed to Ochana Castle. The three of us had stayed silent as my mind raced with everything I had learned the previous twelve hours or so. Rylan's parting words to me were to be ready first thing in the morning, Jericho was to train with me before the council met. Jericho, the Woland scared me to the core.

I threw my legs over the side of my bed, stood up straight and stretched. I looked out the huge bay windows that spanned from floor to ceiling in my room. The view was breathtaking. The brilliant stone castle was built at the apex of three mountains, it was one of the few things I remembered from my walk here last night. The sun was barely over the mountains yet as the sky portrayed a pattern of purple shades. My room opened up to the side that overlooked the main town, which seemed to be bustling already with activity. Even from my height and distance, I could see others start to prepare for their day. Some kind of market appeared to line the main street. Assorted carts and stands were filled with a variety of items for sale. The dragons below continued on with their daily life, a feeling of home sickness washed through me. How I wished I was home with my mom and dad, sitting in my familiar seat at the table as my mom cooked and dad watched the news.

Suddenly, a knock on the door got my attention, as I turned to answer, the door slammed open. I jumped back in surprise. In walked a young woman with Jericho on her heels.

"My Prince," the young woman bowed to me. "My name is Mira, I have been assigned to you, anything you need or want please let me know." She tilted her head to acknowledge the looming man behind her, "Councilman Jericho, has arrived, he insisted in joining me to wake you." She pursed her lips, "And Queen Sila has ordered clothes for you. They shall arrive later this afternoon."

Assigned to me? Like an assistant? At least she seemed to feel the same way towards Jericho as I did. I would have to pick her brain later about the ins and outs of Ochana. I watched as Mira set up a bedside breakfast for me, with more food than I could ever eat by myself. I glanced at the large variety of nourishments, every bit looked amazing. The smell that surrounded me made my stomach growl. She was a quick little thing, she darted around the table getting things situated for me. I noticed Jericho out of my peripheral vision, he watched me as I observed the scene before me. He made me uncomfortable. I needed a distraction, so I looked around the room for my backpack; I needed to get ready for whatever Jericho had in store for me.

I spotted my bag in a nearby chair, the chair looked to be ancient, probably worth more than a car. I went over to grab my bag and searched for a place to change. Mira must have noticed my confused expression when I found no other doors within my spacious bedroom. She walked over to a bookcase and pressed her hand to the side of it. The bookcase open into what looked like a bathroom.

"My Prince, you will find most doors in the castle are hidden. It was designed that way to keep the royal family safe."

Safe? This seems like a pretty extreme security measure. Was I in danger? Mira must have noticed the look on my face, or could read minds like Sila.

"We no longer have a need for such security measures, do not worry. However, the Woland guard has insisted we leave the measure in place." Mira glanced over at Jericho as she spoke. She turned back to me, giving me her full attention.

"Your breakfast is ready, is there anything else I could help you with?" She bounced on her toes as she waited for my response.

I shook my head, I hadn't had a chance to fully wake, and the man in the room made me nervous. I wanted to get this morning over with. Mira bowed towards me before she let herself out. I looked at Jericho over my shoulder, the man's eyes bored into me.

"Oh um, I am just going to change real quick, umm feel free to have some breakfast." I mumbled. Not my finest moment, but it was all I could muster around the man.

I sprinted into the bathroom and turned to close the door when I remembered I had no idea how too. I heard a sigh, then what sounded like a tap on the wall. The bookcase closed with a thud. I changed and cleaned up as fast as I could, I needed to take a shower but the last thing I wanted was to make Jericho wait. I stood in front of the wall where the door should be, and contemplated a moment what my next move should be, I sighed, knocked on the wall and waited. Almost instantly, it opened, and Jericho stood in the doorway with his red eyes that seemed to have the ability to glare into my soul.

I scooted around him and bee lined for the table. I scanned the assorted foods, it was more than one person could possibly eat, many of the foods I had never seen before. I grabbed a mug of coffee, even though I detested the stuff-that's how badly I needed a jolt to wake up. I piled a plate high with pancakes and bacon and smothered them with syrup, the other foods on the table were unfamiliar. As wonderful as it all smelled, I wasn't in the mood to try something new. I shoveled the food in my mouth as fast as I could, aware of the silent man with a permanent scowl behind me. I finished in record time, I turned to look at Jericho. He raised his eyebrows at me, his first sign of emotion. I had no idea if he was amused or frustrated with me.

"So, what's the plan this morning?" I asked with caution.

Jericho shook his head at me and walked to the door. "You failed your first lesson." The sound of his voice surprised me, I had started to think he was mute.

He pinned me with his eyes as I registered what he had just said to me. *Failed?* What was the lesson? "I don't understand? How could I fail? We haven't done anything yet." My voice was laced with confusion.

"I have been charged with the responsibility to prepare you to be a protector. Do you understand the importance of that role?" His brows drew together, almost like he was disgusted with me. "You let a strange woman into your bedchamber, you asked no questions, and ate the food she left behind, food you left unattended with a man you do not trust. Your list of transgressions is endless." He cocked his head, "You are the Prince of Ochana, first lesson; everyone is your enemy." Jericho took one last look at me and stormed from my room.

Second impression of the man went no better than the first. I sat back down on my bed and contemplated Jericho's words. I hung my head and rubbed the back of my neck with my hand. Well, two things stood out the most to me, my new role as Prince of Ochana, and the importance of being a protector. *As an alleged Prince*, I knew nothing about royalty or duties, but enemies? I didn't even know where to start. Was I in danger? In fear, I dropped my hands and fisted them in the sheets beneath. Then there was the whole protector thing, I had no idea how to be a protector, and wasn't sure exactly what I was supposed to protect. Rylan told me a protector protected all that was true, but it made no sense to me. It seemed I had much to learn, and many questions to ask.

But first I needed to find Rylan or Sila and meet with the council. I'm sure they assumed Jericho was escorting me there since I was supposed to be with him. I let out a harsh breath, then again Jericho probably ran right to Rylan and told him all about my failure. *More proof of my weakness.*

I shook my head, I needed to get out of this funk and start being the dragon Rylan was so sure I was. I picked myself up off the bed and walked to the door, which thankfully had been left open after

Jericho's hasty departure. I peeked out the door and looked both ways down the hall. This castle was so huge, I couldn't see and end on either side. I went with my gut and turned right. I had only walked for a few minutes when I ran right into Mira as she emerged from one of those hidden doorways.

"My Prince, you scared me," she grabbed at her chest and let out a gasp. "Do you need anything?" She straightened her back as her wide platinum eyes studied me.

"I am looking for my parents." I asked cautiously as I remembered what Jericho had said about everyone being my enemy.

"The King and Queen are in the throne room meeting with Ochanans as they do each morning. I can show you there?" She smiled at me as she twisted her hands, it seemed the girl couldn't stand still.

"That would be great," I held my hand out for her to go first. "Lead the way." As I followed behind her I thought about what Jericho had told me. I didn't know this girl at all, and even though she seemed harmless, I didn't know anything about dragons, or Siens, as I deduced based on Mira's eyes. With that thought, her silver eyes turned towards me, making me wonder again if she could read my mind like Sila.

"My Prince, I have waited many years for your arrival. It is an honor to be placed with you." She paused and twirled her almost black hair. "You arrived just last night, you must have many questions." She turned back around and continued down the never ending hallway.

"Can you show me how to open the doors and maybe how to find them?" I knew there were much more important questions I should ask, but I had begun to feel trapped.

Mira stopped and looked at the wall, she hesitated a moment before she replied. "Of course, my Prince." She placed her hands on the side of a fancy light. "Look here," she pointed at some kind of small picture right under the light. "This is the royal insignia, they are hidden quite well. Once you get the hang of it though, you will see them everywhere.

They symbolize an exit or entrance." She pushed on the image and the wall shifted, opening up to another hallway. "Press down lightly on the insignia, ask your mahier for entrance, and the wall will open."

She had made it sound simple. Only problem was, I didn't know how to ask my mahier anything. I didn't want to explain my weakness to Mira, so I shook my head in acknowledgement and continued to walk behind her. I would practice later when I got back to my room alone.

Finally, we turned and entered into a room with tall double doors. I looked around to see that we were in a great hall of sorts. The room was much larger than the council room and much more decorative. It also seemed more formal, large crystal chandeliers were suspended from a tall, gold leafed ceiling with pristine tapestries that covered each archway. On the far end of the room, a long line of people stood below three thrones. Rylan and Sila occupied the mounted space near the impressive gold and gem covered thrones. They seemed to be in a deep discussion with Allas. This, I felt, must be the throne room.

Mira paused and looked at me. "Here we are, My Prince, is there anything else you need?"

"I'm good now. Thanks Mira." I watched as she bowed to me and walked away. I hesitated a moment before I began to walk towards Rylan and Sila. I kept to the outskirts of the room in hopes no one would notice me. I passed suits of armor, each one polished perfectly. Grasped in the hands of each knight was a different weapon from the last. As I reached closer to the thrones, I could hear murmurs reverberate around me. Not sure if no one expected me to join, or if they hadn't known I'd arrived.

Sila noticed me first. She walked over and held her hand out for me to grab. I glanced at her hand and wavered a moment, I wished it was my mom Ella's hand, I wanted to go home. Finally, I reached out and clasped her hand, she pulled me towards the front of the room. "Good morning my son, what a pleasant surprise, I wasn't expecting to see you until after morning rounds?" She looked over her shoulder at me with what looked to be a genuine smile.

I was distracted with the murmurs and stares that I almost forgot to respond to Sila. "I uh, didn't know where the council room was. Mira, she um told me you would be here." I looked around the room and caught more than a few surprised looks at my presence.

"I'm glad you found us. We just finished here. We will take the scenic route there so you can see Ochana during daylight." She waved to the crowd that had formed near us in just the past moment, and guided me through another door behind the thrones. Rylan followed behind us with Allas.

Rylan's large hand fell on my shoulder, "Son, I hope you slept well. How did your morning go with Jericho?" I said nothing. Rylan continued. "I have been anticipating his report."

I had no idea what to say to him. Rylan sounded sure that my lesson with Jericho would be nothing but successful. He already sounded proud of me.

Jericho had informed me that I failed. I couldn't tell Rylan that. I started to give an excuse for my failure when we were interrupted. Two men barreled towards us, they looked frantic. I was instantly on alert.

"King Rylan." Two Wolands who wore military uniforms appeared before us, they bowed before they continued. "We need you in the command center."

"We've had a breach!" Both Wolands looked at each other then back to Rylan, as they attempted to catch their breath.

Before Rylan could respond, we were surrounded by guards, they shouted orders out to each other. They demanded we get to safety immediately. I had a guard on either side of me, they pulled me towards the castle. Rylan and Sila were being pulled in the opposite direction. *What was going on?*

"Wait, I need to go with my parents.....hold up." I tried to remove the guards from my arms, but my efforts were useless, they just held on tighter and moved faster.

A loud whistle pierced the air, everyone went silent and turned to find Jericho. "Rylan, Sila you need to go to the bunker now, I will make contact when it's secure." He pushed a bag into Rylan's arms and nodded, a serious look passed between them. "Prince, you will be escorted to a different bunker. We need to separate our two successors for the protection of Ochana." He gave me a no-nonsense look and turned to my guards. "Stay with the Prince, do not leave his side for any reason. Then he turned to me and said in very concise words. "Trust these three. None others."

With those orders we were off.

J.A. Culican

Chapter Eight

We rushed towards the castle. As we were just about to reach the front, the guards pulled me to the right. It looked as though we were going to run right into the side of the mountain, I closed my eyes tight right before impact. The collision I had braced myself for never happened. Instead I found myself inside a cave at the foot of the mountain. I looked over my shoulder a little startled, just in time to see the mountainside close, and trap us inside.

"This way My Prince, we must hurry." One of the guards insisted as he pulled me along.

We began to run. It felt like forever. After we turned a corner for the tenth time, I lost count. If I had to do it alone, there would be no way I'd find my way out of this cave. Not that I could even open the doors that opened and closed as we darted past them to some unknown destination. First thing I had to do when we got out of here was to figure out how to use my mahier, then I needed to find myself a map of Ochana.

Finally, we stopped. I looked around and found myself in a small room, I assumed somewhere in the middle of the mountain by the amount of time we traveled to get here. I looked around. Two small chairs sat around a small square table while a cot was set up right alongside one of the rock walls. At the foot of the cot, I noticed a box that seemed to house some basic supplies. One of the guards pushed me towards the cot. I sat down and kicked my feet on the dirt floor.

"I'll take the first shift." The oldest of the three guards affirmed with the other two before he stepped out of the room. The door slammed shut behind him before either of the other two guards could respond.

I looked over at the two Wolands that were left with my care. They watched me in silence. I instantly felt unnerved by the attention I received from the two. I broke eye contact with them and drifted my eyes around the room, but there was nothing to see.

I looked back at the guards, "How long do you think we will have to stay here?"

"Until it's safe." Guard number one responded.

"Yeah, I know that. But how long does it normally take? I mean, I'm sure you guys have security breaches all the time." Once Jericho gave the orders, the guards acted immediately, they all knew where to go and what they had to do. This was obviously something they were used to.

"The last breach was almost ten years ago and it was a false alarm. You may as well get comfortable, My Prince. My guess is we will be here awhile. For security reasons, you will be the last one released." The two guards looked at each other, then turned and faced the wall where the door was. They looked to be in serious guard mode, they stood ramrod straight, chins held high, with their hands behind their backs. I guess that was my cue, talk time was over.

***

I counted the crevices in the rock ceiling above the cot around a hundred times. I wish I knew what was going on. My guards haven't said a single word to me since our earlier conversation. The oldest guard returned a while ago and another guard took his place outside our room.

Suddenly, a knock echoed through the room. The two remaining guards stood up even straighter and reached for the door. The wall slid open to an imposing figure. I couldn't see over the guards' heads to see who was there. I assumed since no weapons were drawn and no dragons appeared our visitor was a friendly. The guards stepped to the side and Jericho moved forward. He was followed by my other guard.

"We need to go, My Prince." Jericho commanded. Before I could react, he was out of the room.

I jumped off the cot and raced after him. No way was I letting him out of my sight. Jericho rushed through the caves, I had to speed up my usual pace double time just to keep up with him. He seemed more uptight than normal. His jaw was clamped shut and his eyes focused directly ahead. His normal glares towards me were surprisingly missing. I wondered what had happened. Had we really been breached? If so, by who?

"Answers will be given in due time. We are meeting with the council now." His steely eyes finally turned to me, I thought I saw relief there for just a slight second. "Second lesson, pay close attention to each and every person in the room, do not let your guard down for anyone. You and I will debrief afterwards with your thoughts." With that he turned away from me and picked up his pace even faster.

After some time, we arrived in front of the council room. As we entered through the iron doors, which were flanked by two new Woland soldiers, I noticed everyone was seated around the table. Huge screens that I had not seen when I was there last were placed in the middle of the table, others seemed to be placed flat on the elegant table. I couldn't see what was on the screens, but everyone's attention was focused on them. No one even noticed our arrival. It gave me a chance to take in the new faces that had joined us. It looked like two more Wolands and one Leslo.

"Micah, Nico why are you away from command?" Jericho glowered at the two Wolands awaiting a response.

"Sir, we have news. We knew you would want the information immediately."

"Why did you not call to me, Nico? Jericho's temper was starting to show.

"Sir we did, you did not respond." Both Wolands looked at Jericho with caution.

Jericho's body stiffened. Only I could tell due to my proximity to him; no one else around would have any idea as his expression never altered. I looked back at the Wolands in anticipation, awaiting their news. They stayed silent.

"Get on with it, we have much to discuss." Jericho spat.

The blond haired Woland, Nico cleared his throat, obviously affected by Jericho's tone. "Sir, we know who the Woland was," he paused and looked over at his partner, with a look of help. Jericho's eyes followed his line of sight.

"It was Cairo sir, he had a dramon girl with him...." Micah looked down before he finished his sentence. He looked uncomfortable.

Rylan's voiced boomed from across the room, "Impossible! No dramon can enter Ochana." His fists pounded on the table.

Nico bowed towards Rylan, "My King, our surveillance video caught his attempt at entering. The dramon girl was in a shift I have never seen before; she was flying on her own."

"How is that possible, dramons don't possess mahier? Are you sure she was a dramon?" Rylan sounded unsure. His gaze settled on the council for answers.

"Never in our history has a dramon been able to wield our mahier, they aren't strong enough." Allas stated as she looked around the table as she shook her head in surprise.

"Before we go any further, Micah, pull up the video, we need to determine if the girl was indeed a dramon." Jericho strode across the room, placed his hands on the table and leaned over one of the monitors that was built into the table. He looked up at Micah, "Now!"

Micah scrambled over to another monitor, his hands flew across the screen in search of the video in question. I wandered my way over to where Rylan and Sila stood, I placed myself on the right side of Sila and looked down at the screen in wait. Sila place her hand on my shoulder in a sign of comfort. Everyone stayed silent.

The screens came to life after just a few moments. At first all I could see were the clouds that concealed Ochana. Out of the bottom right corner of the screen a huge red dragon, a Woland became visible. I heard Sila whisper the name "Cairo," no one else made a noise as we all continued to watch. Cairo's whole body became visible in the screen, just as a reddish orange dragon like creature flew in view behind him. The girl had scales that covered a human looking body, with large goldish red wings that flapped from her back, as she flew closer, her eyes glowed gold.

My breath caught in my throat. I couldn't believe it. I knew that girl. I looked around the room to see if anyone else had the same revelation as me. She looked so different from the last time I saw her not more than six weeks ago. My eyes were glued to the screen, I begged my eyes to see something different, someone different. Both Cairo and the girl's heads suddenly looked up, they were regarding something over the camera, out of view. Quickly, both of them spun around and took off in the other direction. I continued to watch as what looked to be around twenty Wolands took chase after them.

Everyone continued to stare at the screen, there was nothing left but clouds. I inhaled a deep breath and looked up. Jericho stood across from me, his eyes pinned me in place. He hastily shook his head at me and looked away. I was confused. Did he want me to stay quiet about what I saw? How would that even be possible with at least two dragons here who could read my mind?

"Dramons can't fly or shift. What was that?" Rylan looked around, "Have we made contact with Cairo?" No one answered.

"Answer your King!" Jericho roared with a slam of his hands on the table.

Micah's eyes swung to Rylan's, "We lost them, My King. We have been trying to call for him, he hasn't answered yet."

"Get back to command, I will speak to you both later." Jericho dismissed them without looking up from the screen.

The wall slammed shut with their departure, shaking everyone awake from what they just witnessed. Everyone started to speak at once. I tried to keep up with the conversations around me, but it was impossible, my own mind raced with what I had just seen. I took a step back and observed everyone, just as Jericho had instructed me to do. Everyone seemed on edge except for Sila. She was still focused on the screen.

Sila finally looked up from the screen. Her eyes scanned the faces around the table, everyone paused as her eyes hit them, she had the room's full attention now. "Something feels wrong; Cairo is one of our most loyal Wolands. For him to bring that creature to Ochana, he's either in trouble or she is important. We must find him, he must know we do not intend to harm him or the girl."

"Why would they run if they weren't here to harm us?" Jules' blue eyes looked worried as she addressed the table. "And the girl, she was no dragon, we should not concern ourselves with her well-being."

"Regardless, we need to talk to her either way, she was able to get to close to Ochana for us not to be concern by her. As for what she is, we don't know if she is a dragon or not. We need to find them both, Jericho, make sure every available Woland understands the importance of finding Cairo and the girl, alive." Sila punctuated the word *alive*, leaving no room for a misunderstanding.

An unknown voice broke the trance between Sila and Jericho. "My Queen, King," The new Leslo bowed to Rylan and Sila. "I am concerned with the wellbeing of Prince Colton. He has been in Ochana less than twenty-four hours and we have already had a breach. It could very well be unrelated, but we cannot be sure of it."

Every eye turned to me like I would have the answer to that. I tried with all my might not to think what was really going through my head. I mean I knew the mysterious girl, I've known her for what seemed like forever. It couldn't be a coincidence even though I prayed it was.

"Little brother, good point." Rylan nodded towards, *my uncle?* "Jericho, step up security around the Prince. He is to never be alone. We must not underestimate Cairo and the girl. We need to find the two now." Rylan looked towards the rest of the council. "As for the rest of you, we must proceed with inducting Prince Colton to Ochana. We will not let this breach discourage us, his training will continue as planned. I expect my son to be ready in four weeks to start with the new protectors."

That caught my attention, it had been brought to my attention a few times on the importance of being a protector and that I would be one. I was still unsure as to what I would be protecting however. An induction was news to me. Induction into what, I wondered. I needed time with Sila, mostly because she seemed the least threatening of my two parents. I had yet to have more than five minutes alone with either of my parents since we arrived, It was important I found time soon.

"I agree My King," Jericho looked to each council member. "We need to pick up our schedule with the

Prince, each of us must work with him each day. As for security, I will bring our Prince with me to command and select two personal guards. It will be a good opportunity for the Prince to see our Wolands in action."

"Good, we will meet again tomorrow. I expect we will have news on Cairo by then." Rylan's words came out more as a threat than a command. "Also, I expect reports from each of you on your plans to train the Prince."

Rylan stood and walked to the door with Sila close behind. They left me with the council, and my apparent uncle. I looked to Jericho for direction. He stood and glared at my uncle, waiting for him to look his way.

Jericho locked eyes with my uncle, "Prince Zane, a word."

He nodded and the two walked to the other side of the room. I was unable to hear what they talked about, but it seemed by the looks they gave to each other it was not a pleasant conversation. Both men were wound tight, they glared at each other as they spoke. Jericho broke from the conversation and walked towards me.

"My Prince, let's go."

Jericho never broke stride as he walked right by me. It was clear he expected me to follow him without question, and by the man's expression there was no way I was going too. With purpose he walked up to two guards that stood outside the main council room entrance.

"Watch him," was all he said before he headed towards the command center.

J.A. Culican

Chapter Nine

We walked to the command center in complete silence. Mere steps in front of me, Jericho vibrated with anger. I had so many questions but was afraid to utter a sound at the irate man ahead of me. The walk ended quickly. We reached a set of stairs that Jericho bounded up, I followed him up and we arrived at a circular glass building. It didn't seem to fit in with the rest of Ochana. I stared at it in wonder until I realized Jericho had a glow in his eyes as he glared at me. He looked down at me over his shoulder.

"The lesson continues. Don't say or touch anything." He didn't wait for me to reply. Instead, he turned and stomped through the doors.

As we entered the building, the chatter and murmurs in the background completely fell silent. Every eye turned towards Jericho. I shrank away from him not wanting the attention placed on me. I gazed around the ginormous room, made to feel even bigger by the glass walls, there looked to be around fifty men and women scattered about as they completed their duties. I watched as the two Wolands closest to me typed away on one of the most high tech looking computers I had ever seen. They were almost completely surrounded by monitors that depicted a series of numbers and letters I had no idea how to read. A few looked familiar, I noticed the two men who left the council room earlier and my three guards from our lock down.

"My office, now," he addressed a fellow Woland, who seemed unaffected by Jericho's sour mood. The Woland was taller than Jericho, with almost white hair and oversized red eyes. "I want every bit of information we have." He turned to leave, but right before he entered what I assumed was his office, he turned and addressed everyone. "We will get Cairo and that girl, by nightfall. Alive. No excuses."

I ran after him before he closed the door, I still had no idea if I would be able to open it once it closed. As I entered, Jericho pointed to a chair while he scowled at the man in front of him. I took my cue and had a seat. No way did I want those eyes trained on me.

"When did he return?" the glass walls shook with the strength of his voice.

"He arrived right before the breach sir. With all that was going on, he slipped right past us." The man never took his eyes from Jericho's.

"Unacceptable. He is a threat. You know that. How many eyes do we have on him?"

"Four, as you commanded."

"Full reports, every hour. Do you understand?"

"Yes, sir. I will check in with the team now."

Jericho waved the man out and impaled me with his eyes. I had no idea how the other man was able to stare him in the eyes without fear. I tried to understand what I had just witnessed. I figured they were talking about my Uncle Zane; however, I had no idea why, I knew nothing about him. I hadn't even known he existed until a few minutes ago.

"Speak, tell me everything." His voice came off so much more calm, it took me by surprise.

I wasn't sure what he wanted me to speak about, there seemed to be an endless amount of things we needed to discuss. The breach, Cairo, the girl. Then there was the topic of my alleged uncle. Not to mention the hundred or so questions I had about everything else. I looked at Jericho for guidance, could he be more specific?

"We will speak of all of it. First, the girl. Who is she?" He remained still, and I remained unfamiliar to this kind of behavior from him.

"I think...I think she is my best friend." I stared at the ground as I spoke. I wasn't sure how much to tell him. I didn't want him or anyone to hurt her. "She doesn't have a mean bone in her body, there is no way she was here to harm anyone." I finally looked up at Jericho, I hoped he saw how honest I was being.

"Do you know what she is?"

"No, I've never seen her that way. I don't know what happened to her." As I thought about it, she would be just as surprised to know what I have become.

"This girl, your best friend, attempted to enter Ochana, just a few hours after your arrival. Only the council was aware of your arrival until this morning. Think Cole, what could she want?"

I was caught off guard, it was the first time he had called me by my name, actually it was the first time anyone had called me Cole. I had no idea why she would be here, she never said anything to me about being different, but neither did I to her. Wait, I didn't know I was a dragon until just last night, maybe she just found out about herself too. As the thought sprouted from my head, I looked to Jericho. He nodded his head in agreement.

"You could very well be right. But that doesn't answer the question as to why she was here and why she was with a loyal Woland." He stood and started to pace the length of the room.

Again, I wished I could read minds like most of the other Dragons. I could only imagine the thoughts that were inside Jericho's head at the moment, as I watched him pace from one side of the room to the other. He stopped by the large glass wall that overlooked the edge of Ochana. The view was a picturesque setting of endless clouds, clouds for as far as you could see. He stood there for what felt like forever in silence.

"Your friend, what is her name?" His words expelled in a thoughtful tone.

I didn't want to tell him, I was scared for her. "I-"

He turned to face me, "Her parents, what are their names?"

"Umm, I don't know. I met her when she moved in with her grandparents. I was only ten or so."

Truth is she never spoke of her parents, I don't even know what happened to them, if anything.

Jericho was quiet for a bit as he processed this bit of information. "Do you know where she would go? Some place she would feel safe?"

I knew exactly where she would go, where we both had gone many times whenever we needed to get away. It was our place. But if she knew I was here, would she go there? The thought popped into my head before I could stop it, I still didn't trust Jericho completely and I didn't want him to hurt her. I peered up at him and held my breath as I waited.

"Good, trust will be earned. I will not hurt your friend. I want her alive, I am very curious about her and need to know why she came here. Now, tell me about this place." Again, his eyes pinned me to my seat.

"It's silly." I paused to look out the wall over Jericho's shoulder, I knew I didn't have a choice, but I didn't want to tell him. "When we were around ten we found an old hunting cabin between our houses. It looked like it had been abandoned for years."

"Tell me more, why would she go there?"

"It was our safe haven of sorts. Whenever we needed a break from the real world we would go there. No one else but the two of us knew of it, at least no one ever let on that they knew about it." Memories sped through my mind. When we were younger we spent all our free time there. Once we got older and busier, we would go, but not usually together.

"We will leave within the hour. You will bring me to this cabin of yours."

Jericho left no room for argument. I just hoped she was smart enough not to go there. If she knew I was here, she would know that the first place I would look for her was there. Unless she wanted me to find her. I paused with that thought and peeked over at Jericho, he tapped on some sort of screen on his desk, he was completely engrossed and paid no mind to me. Did she want me to find her? Maybe she was in trouble.

Another thought popped into my head and before I could stop my mouth I spit out the question to Jericho. "Why don't you trust Zane?"

His eyes flashed from his screen to me, "You will find that there is much for you to learn. Like I told you before, everyone is your enemy."

"You included?" Darn my mouth, though Jericho didn't seem phased by my question.

"Everyone."

He punctuated the word in a way to end my questions. His eyes once again found the screen, putting a halt to any further conversation. What would happen when we got to the cabin? What if she wasn't there? Based on Jericho's expression, he seemed sure she would be.

Jericho stood from his desk, throwing the screen he had in his hand down onto his desk and walked to the door. He paused and looked over his shoulder at me. "I don't believe in coincidences. She will be there. If she is truly as close to you as you claim, she will know that is the first place you will have thought about. She wants us to find her and she knows you won't hurt her." He walked out the door and headed towards the same Woland he had yelled at before.

I followed behind him. In my head, I replayed what he had just said to me. Did she really want me to find her? He was right, I would never hurt her, no matter what she was or what her reason for coming here was. I had tuned out everything around me until I heard a loud crash and Jericho's voice as he yelled at a group of Wolands.

"What do you mean gone? Where were you?" He turned towards the poor Woland that he seemed to always be mad at. "Garrik find him. Now." He took off towards the door we had entered earlier, at least five Wolands chased after him. Once back outside, Jericho raced towards the castle, the Wolands hot on his heels. I ran after them, not knowing exactly what was going on. I guessed they had lost track of Zane, he seemed to get the most heated when it came to him. Jericho stormed through the front entrance, the guards parted in his wake without hesitation. He continued down the long hall. Unlike me, he knew his way around the castle. I was lost.

Finally, we turned into a familiar room, the throne room. Jericho continued to stomp his way to the front where Rylan and Sila were seated. He had no care for the dragons around him. His entourage of Wolands stayed close behind him. When Jericho reached the front of the room, he bowed to Rylan and Sila. I was too far away to hear what was said between them. Rylan stood suddenly and stormed to the exit behind the thrones, Sila and the Wolands followed. I ran to catch up with them.

Once the door shut behind me, Rylan bellowed with anger, "What do you mean gone?" He looked between everyone present. "Find him."

"My King, I can promise you we will find him." Jericho held Rylan's attention. "We have a lead on the girl. Prince Colton is needed in order to capture the girl securely. I ask that you allow him to join us on our mission."

Rylan swung his eyes in my direction. I could see the indecision there. "His safety is in your hands Jericho. Bring my son back unharmed."

"You have my word, My King, I will protect him with my life." He bowed to Rylan and Sila and gestured to the rest of us to follow him.

As I passed by Rylan he stopped me, "Be safe my son, trust Jericho and do as he says."

I nodded as I trailed behind the Wolands. Once outside, Jericho started to bark orders at everyone. It seemed these were the Wolands that would join us on our journey. He expected us to arrive to Clover by nightfall. I thought about the trip I took with Rylan and Sila, I hadn't flown the whole way, I had hitched a ride on the back of Rylan. It was the only time I had flown, and it was a much shorter trip than the one Jericho had planned.

We headed to the exact spot we had landed my first night in Ochana, when the council had accepted me. The Wolands around me started to transform into their dragons. I stood still, evened out my breathing and attempted to call for my dragon. I was way too nervous around the others to change, I didn't even feel a twinge.

"Men, go ahead, we will follow behind." Jericho shouted to his men as he walked towards me. He looked down at me with a slight frown. "You need to shift, the men are gone. They are aware that you have just found your dragon. There is no reason to be nervous." He turned and shifted rapidly into his dragon. If I had blinked, I would've missed it completely.

Jericho was massive, and even bigger than Rylan, though much leaner. His scales were a dark red, almost black, his eyes were the same menacing red that glowed when angry, and right now they glowed deep red my way. I took a deep breath and closed my eyes. I needed to find my dragon and fast. I pictured myself in my dragon form, with my colorful scales, wide wings, and frightening claws. The shift started unexpectedly, it seemed much quicker than before, but still much longer than Jericho's. The wind was taken from me as my wings broke free, pushing me to the ground. I looked up to see Jericho, his eyes were no longer glowing, but he seemed unsettled.

"Stay close."

The vibration from Jericho's voice shook me as I watched him propel from the ground and take off. I exhaled as I followed his lead, praying I'd make it to Clover in one piece, and that Eva would be found safe when I got there.

Chapter Ten

The wind whooshed around me as we flew over the Lincoln Sea towards Ellesmere Island. Thanks to the light and the time of day, I was able to take a better look around me, than the last time I took this journey. The scenery was something out of a fairy tale. The clouds were smooth and crisp as they floated around me unbothered by the mammoth sized dragons speeding through them. The sea was a light shade of blue almost white and frozen in most areas, I had never seen anything like it.

Jericho stayed close to me as we flew, I could feel the impatience radiate off him with how slow our pace was. I tried to fly as fast as I could; however, no matter how much I was able to pick up my speed, they all flew faster. It was clear by how easy the flight seemed to be for everyone else that they were used too much quicker speeds. I finally got into a good groove when I realized the Wolands ahead of me started to descend. I followed their lead. As I neared the ground I sent a silent prayer up that I wouldn't tumble when I landed like the last time. The dragons around me were fierce warriors, I paled in comparison. Even though I was new to being a dragon. If I crashed and burned, there'd be no way they'd think high of me.

Finally, my feet hit the ground with a powerful thud, my firm claws dug into the snow which kept me upright, I exhaled in a sign of relief. The Wolands all gathered around Jericho and I, some had shifted to their human counterparts, while others stayed as dragons. Jericho was in his human form, and luckily, he didn't seem angry anymore.

"You have fifteen minutes. Eat and meet back here." With no question, the five Wolands took off in search of food with Jericho's words. "Have you hunted in your dragon form?"

I was the only one left so it was clear Jericho was speaking to me. I've done a whole lot of nothing besides fly to Ochana in my dragon form.

Jericho shook his head. "This ought to be interesting. Let your dragon lead. Use your instincts. Follow me." He mouthed to me.

Jericho swiftly morphed into his Woland. It amazed me how fluid and inherent his shifts were. He pushed off the ground with ease and started for the tree line. I was able to follow, but my moved were much more chaotic. I swayed back and forth, and had no handle on my position. I began to wonder what we were going to hunt. Last time I was here, I didn't see any animals, but Rylan did feed us some kind of meat. Back when I lived with my actual dad, he would take me hunting every year, deer season being his favorite.

"Muskox, to your right."

I shifted my head and saw a herd of something. The animals had thick black coats, curved horns that bulged from their heads and a horrible odor emitted from afar. Muskox. I had never seen anything like them, we definitely didn't have these back in Texas.

"Descend quickly, grab one and keep going. The ox expect to be hunted by dragons, so they will run if they catch you."

I watched as Jericho swooped quickly towards the herd. He snatched one of the muskox with his large jaw and kept flying, as he circled back around to where we had originally landed. Somehow, I thought my experience with hunting would be helpful in this situation, but I couldn't be more wrong, hunting with a bow and hunting with my mouth were two completely different tasks.

I braced myself for the inevitable and took off towards the herd. One muskox was off to the side alone, he was occupied as he nibbled on a piece of plant sticking up through the snow, I targeted on him. Just as Jericho had, I swooped down towards the muskox. Right before I reached him, his head popped up and looked directly at me. He took off at full speed, he moved much faster than I had expected. His rapid movement caught the attention of the rest of the herd and they all took off. Out of my peripheral, I saw what looked like the biggest muskox of the group. Abruptly, he started to charge in my direction. I wasn't in the mood to fight him off, so I swooped back up and headed towards Jericho, empty-handed.

The five Wolands stood by Jericho and watched me return. I could see the laughter in their eyes as I approached, but none of them said anything to me about what they just witnessed. My feet hit the ground. Thankfully I didn't fall forward. Jericho walked towards me.

"Good, I've never met a dragon who successfully caught a muskox their first time. You were close." He gave a quiet chuckle, a laughter so faint, I am pretty sure I wouldn't have even heard it in my human form. "Help yourself to the leftovers, we are leaving in five minutes."

I wished he had warned me about that little tidbit of information before I attempted to catch a muskox, maybe then I wouldn't have felt like such a failure. It seemed these dragons were all about making the new dragons feel foolish, or maybe it was just me. I walked over to the remains of the leftover muskox. It smelled putrid. I wrinkled my nose and gave it a go anyway. I'd never had raw meat before, but I guess a dragon always ate that way, based on what I saw of the other dragons around me. It actually tasted good. So good, I finished off the rest of the scraps.

The Wolands began to snicker at me. I was just about to open my mouth in defense, but they briskly shifted into their dragons. It was probably better off that way. I felt the rumble of Jericho's voice before I actually heard it.

"There is always a first time, why not get it out of the way. Next time you'll be ready." Without waiting for a response he took off towards the sky.

I guess he had a point. With that thought I took off immediately after him. I felt a little better. The longer we flew, the more in control of my dragon I felt. It was like my dragon and I just needed time to bond and get to know each other. It was such a strange feeling, my dragon. I thought it would be like to separate beings, me and my dragon, but it wasn't like that at all, he was a part of me, like an arm or a leg, I had a dragon. I noticed the snow was gone and there were city lights not too far off. Darkness began to creep towards us.

"Stay close, my mahier is protecting you from humans." He paused, "I feel something else watching us."

I flew as close as possible to Jericho. I noticed the other Wolands surrounded us in a protective circle. What could possibly be watching us that would make them all act this way? My eyes searched the space around me; all I could see were clouds and the city as we approached. We started to fly above the clouds, in an attempt to conceal us further. In silence, we flew the rest of the way.

My nerves were completely fried by the time we arrived to Clover. Surprisingly, the familiarity of home did nothing to soothe me. As we descended I realized I didn't fear my landing as I had in the past. It was clear the longer I was in my dragon form the more comfortable I was with trusting its instincts. We landed quietly and shifted back into our human forms right on the outskirts of Eva's grandparents' home. The cabin wasn't far from here; about a five-minute walk. The Woland seemed to be scoping the area out.

"Cairo is here. Let's go."

Jericho took off into the woods. I had no idea how he knew where he was going or that Cairo was here. I felt nothing. The only sounds were the wildlife that encircled us. I could hear a pack of coyotes off in the distance howling at the moon, the sound matched the fear that surrounded me. The Wolands walked in complete silence. My feet were the only ones loud enough to hear as they crunched on the brush under my feet.

Our arrival to the cabin was swift. We stopped about twenty yards from the front door. Without words, the Wolands encircled the small cabin. Once my haven, this one-room, rickety cabin with no electricity or plumbing was the only thing that stood between six powerful Wolands and my best friend.

The front swung open with a loud creak, out came a large man with long brown hair, well past his shoulders and fiery red eyes. *This must be Cairo.* He walked straight to Jericho. He lifted his hands up in a show of peace. He stopped about three feet in front of him and bowed his head, awaiting Jericho to speak.

Jericho spoke slowly and evenly as he punctuated out three small words, "Who is she?"

"She is the one."

"Be more specific!" Jericho's hands rolled into tight fists. "I will charge you with the endangerment of all dragons who call Ochana home-"

"She is the one from Aprella's premonition. The second will show himself soon."

Jericho broke eye contact with Cairo and gaped at me, "Are you sure?" His eyes were still fixed on me.

"Yes, I spent two hundred years studying the book of Aprella before you recruited me to the guard. It was luck I came across her when I did. And you know neither of us believe in luck. I was meant to find her. No other Woland would have known what she was, they would have killed her on sight." Cairo looked over his shoulder just as Eva poked her head through the door.

Jericho looked past Cairo to get a glimpse of her. "Why not come to us with this news? You knew how we would react to your breach."

"That was my plan."

Cairo stepped closer to Jericho and whispered something in his ear, I watched as Jericho's body stiffened. Like a set of dominos, the rest of the Wolands bodies stiffened as they looked to each other. I figured some kind of clairvoyant communication had transpired between them.

"We must get back to Ochana immediately. It is not safe for the girl or the Prince to be out here." Jericho stated with certainty.

"The Prince? I was unaware he had returned, why would you bring him with you?" Cairo seemed confused. "I agree, we need to leave. I had hoped you would come sooner."

Jericho stepped back from Cairo and assessed him. "Why would you come here to an unfamiliar place I know nothing of, if you did not know the Prince was back?" Jericho stepped in front of me in a protective stance as he spoke.

"I called to you and told you where I was. What does the Prince have to do with my location?" Cairo shifted his body until it completely covered the cabin door, effectively blocking our view of Eva.

Jericho cocked his head to the side, "The Prince knows the girl. He identified her to me and brought me here."

Cairo eased up a bit, "Is he-"

Boooom. A loud crash interrupted Cairo. It came from the east, in the exact direction of my parent's house. I started to move to where the explosion occurred, but was stopped short by a hand on my shoulder. I turned to see Jericho, who nodded to his guards and they all took off towards the crash.

"We must go. Now. Get the girl."

Jericho pulled me forward and together we bolted towards the main road. Faintly, I could hear Cairo and Eva tread not far behind us. Finally, we broke through a line of pine trees. Jericho and Cairo promptly morphed into their dragons. I followed their lead. This time, the shift into my reptilian state was brisk. I barely thought about it. I rotated my head to look at Eva. She had already shifted too. My initial glimpse of dragon Eva was only through security cameras back at Ochana. Now, I could see the intricate details of her golden scales. They gleamed a magnificent gold and practically covered her entire body. She was a vision with her golden wings with amber gold feathers.

"We must fly fast, straight to Ochana. Do not stop for anything."

Jericho's eyes blazed a fiery glow as his voice bounced around in my head. I think he expected a fight from me, and I almost put one up, until I heard another loud crash that sounded nearby. It felt like the large pine trees were being uprooted from the ground and catapulted into the distance. Whatever was causing the noise, I knew I was no match for it. I hoped the Wolands ensures my parents were safe, and kept them that way.

"Their first goal is to keep you safe. Only then will they check on your parents. They aren't here for them, they want the two of you. Let's go."

I hoped Jericho was right. If I brought any troubles to my parents, I couldn't live with myself. Eva stood close to me, she placed one of her golden-scaled hands on my shoulder, almost like she didn't believe I was real. I knew how she felt as I took her in next to me. Everything felt surreal.

Jericho led us into the sky as Cairo positioned behind us. We traveled fast, much quicker than we did on our way here. Eva seemed to have no problem keeping up with us. She was so small next to us, almost like a pixie amongst giants. Only, we were dragons, and she was...?

Chapter Eleven

I landed on Ochana with a bang. As soon as my feet hit the ground, my entire body thrust forward and my upper half smacked full force into the hard terrain. I was exhausted. In a flow of delicate grace, Eva made a light-footed land next to me. I was jealous at her ease. Almost immediately, we were encircled by over twenty Wolands. Jericho and Cairo puffed out their chests and positioned for battle. Their dragons were much larger than the Wolands that surrounded us. Jericho and Cairo's dragons frightened the guards, they took a few steps back in horror. Jericho crouched low, ready to pounce at the slightest threat. Every time any of the guards made any kind of movement, both dragons bellowed a deep warning growl.

As exhausted as I was, I scrambled to my feet and stood as tall as I could muster. I shielded Eva with my wings, but she stepped out from my protection. She spread her wings and prepared herself to fight. Without notice, the two guards parted in front of me. Rylan stepped through. He gave me a quick glance, then turned to the Woland guards.

"Your Prince has returned, his mission was to bring Cairo and the girl back. He has completed his first mission with success. Is this the greeting you meet him with? Show your respect. Now." Rylan growled at the guards until they relaxed and bowed their heads my way.

The guards started to shift back to their human forms. Once the Wolands had morphed back, Jericho and Cairo did also. They had waited for all threats to banish first. Cairo stepped up to the other side of Eva, sandwiching her between us. Once Cairo was in place, Jericho turned to Rylan.

"We need to meet with the council immediately, and have Councilwoman Jules bring the book of Aprella." Jericho turned and gestured to the three of us. We morphed back into our human state and followed Jericho through the streaming waterfall.

I was surprised Rylan let Jericho speak that way to him. He didn't ask, he told him what needed to be done and Rylan had accepted it with no question. It either showed that Rylan trusted Jericho, or feared him. The four of us took a seat around the large, polished stone table as we waited for the council to arrive. I watched as Eva inspected the carved images on the wall. We had yet to speak to each other about what was going on. I assumed she was just as confused as me the first time I sat at this table.

"Both."

Jericho's deep voice caught me off guard. I wasn't sure what he meant by *both*, but he looked at me while he said it. He nodded his head at me and turned towards Cairo. He didn't say a word to him, just glared. I wondered if Jericho was probing through Cairo's mind as he often did with me. I thought about what he'd just said to me. It had to be my thought on Rylan, I wondered how Jericho had earned his trust, he was always telling me not to trust anyone.

Suddenly, a commotion erupted outside the council room. Both Cairo and Jericho stood as the whole council barreled into the room. Everyone took their assigned seats, I was already in my seat next to Rylan's, with Eva next to me and Cairo on the other side of her. Jules, the Galian with sapphire eyes, placed a large book in the middle of the council room table. The room fell silent as each attendee gazed at the old and bulky book.

Rylan interrupted the silence. "Explain to me what is going on." His eyes pierced Jericho then flew to Cairo.

"I believe the golden dragon prophecy, is coming true, My King." Cairo bowed his head towards Rylan and nodded towards the book.

"Why now? The prophecy was to come at a time of great fear." Sila questioned.

"What makes you think this girl is the golden dragon?" Rylan challenged as he tilted his head at Eva and squinted as he observed her.

"Aprella's prophecy affirmed that the golden dragon would encompass humanity, therefore they would not take the true shape of a dragon, but one of a human..." Cairo paused and turned to Rylan. "My King, she can wield mahier as only dragons can, but her shape is that of a human."

Jules cleared her throat to get everyone's attention. "It would explain the Prince's coloring." She nodded towards me. "A warrior that is comprised of the four dragon founders would fight by her side." It sounded like Jules was reciting the prophecy from heart.

"We must know for sure." Rylan looked at Jules. "Your Galian Meka, is the Keeper of the Book of Aprella. There must be a way to know for sure."

"It has been many years since I studied that prophecy. If it is true, it means we are in a time of fear. I will speak with Meka."

"You must look into it now and report to the council tomorrow. If it is true, we need to act fast. The last time we were in a time of fear, we lost a great warrior as punishment." Rylan's voice wavered a bit. "Jericho, check in with each Woland guard, we must know if they have encountered anything during their rounds that will back this book's claim."

"Yes, My..."

Cairo interrupted Jericho. "Tonight, My King. We were under attack. The Woland guard that was with us, have we heard from them?"

The whereabouts of the other Wolands completely escaped my mind. Between prophecy, and Eva the golden dragon, I was distracted. I heard the part about the loss of the great warrior during the previous time of fear, and completely sidetracked. I looked over to Jericho, who had somehow found himself a tablet, in which he pressed at irritably. He must know the fate of the other Wolands.

"My King, they are on their way back. The attack had come from a pack of;" his eye brows scrunched in confusion, "Carnites." He turned the tablet screen towards Rylan so he could see the video that played.

Jericho looked up from the tablet, he had a muddled look on his face. I had never seen that much emotion from him. Everyone looked around the table in disbelief. *What were Carnites?*

"You would know them as a mix of trolls and giants, my son. Large beings, highly destructive, though not too bright. We haven't had a sighting of them in many years." She seemed perplexed by the news.

Eva abruptly stood up, causing her chair to skid behind her and tumble to the floor. "Can someone please start from the beginning, I am having a really hard time following all this. What is the book of Aprella, what is the prophecy about and what am I?" She stared confidently at Rylan as she spoke.

Cairo chuckled beside me, "This one is a spitfire, no fear whatsoever."

Sila gestured for Eva to sit back down. She rose and began to pace around the room. "Let's start from the beginning. Not your beginning, but the beginning of all." Sila paused and gazed at the images on the wall. "Aprella was the first ever known dragon. No one knows where she came from or how she came about."

"Most dragons believe she was born from the four elements, with fire being the most dominant." Rylan added.

"My King, this is true. Aprella carried the mahier of all the dragons of today. You could imagine the amount of strength it gave her. She bore four dragon sons, legend has it, she broke off some of her mahier in order to create them. A Galian, a Sien, a Woland and a Leslo, the four founding dragons." Sila gestured around the room at the images that surrounded us as she spoke. "She shared her mahier with her sons in a way that each dragon born would also carry her mahier."

"We all descend from Aprella, she created Ochana. Aprella was gifted with sweeping prophetic visions. She is the only known dragon to possess such power. She could see what would be." Jules seized the book from the center of the council table.

"Everything she saw is inside our book of prophecy. It has yet to be wrong."

"So, what did she write about me?" Eva still sounded strong and sturdy, though quite eager.

"If you are who we think, you are a draman. But a true draman. Other dragons have been described as such, but they are not. They are not like you." A smirk spread across Sila's lips. "You are the golden dragon, the one who will stand by a great warrior and save all that is true. Aprella wrote about you, a girl who was half dragon and half human. She would come in a time of great need, and soon after, a special warrior would be born who embraced the essence of the four founders. Together, the half-dragon girl and great warrior would become The Keeper of Dragons. They would save us all." Sila sat back down with that last sentence, her voice much softer.

I could picture Eva as the girl from Aprella's prophecy that they spoke of. She had always been strong and confident. She picked up new skills with ease. In school, classmates from various groups and cliques flocked to her. She had such a way with people, they all trusted her. I never understood how we became friends, or why she chose to stay my friend through the years. I was nothing like her.

Eva studied me as my thoughts rambled. Her eyes seemed to smile at me even though her mouth didn't move a muscle. "You are much stronger than you think, Cole. When I first moved to Clover, you took me in as a friend. I was an outsider, no one moves to that small Texas town, they are born there. But you, you accepted me from the beginning. That took a lot of guts. A lot of heart, and a lot of true care." She placed her hands on my forearm and smiled. She then turned back to Sila. "What are we saving you from?"

"Everything." Sila looked to Jericho.

"We have been protecting this world from the beginning. Creatures always want to conquer and capture Ochana. For some time, it has weighed heavy on the dragons' shoulders to protect the land, and all that is true. If you both are now in Ochana, our two key fighters, and the prophecy is coming to light, there must be uncovered forces working in darkness. Creatures, like the Carnites, are preparing for war." With each word, Jericho's voice had grown stronger, as if he became more confident as he matched prophecy to the recent events of mine and Eva's arrival to Ochana. "Since the beginning, it has been the Wolands job to protect the land." Jericho bowed towards us. "We will stand alongside the two of you. We will protect you as you protect us."

A warrior. They think I'm the warrior who will save them. Who will protect humans from creatures I don't know anything about? I felt like the time was now to explain to them how weak I was, I mean I failed Jericho's first test. How was I supposed to protect anyone when I couldn't even protect myself?

I also wondered how Eva deciphered my thoughts earlier. Suddenly, I heard a loud giggle. It was Eva. I turned to her. "How?"

"I don't know, it felt like you were screaming it to me. It resounded in my head." She shrugged. "Also, you're wrong about being weak. I promise you."

"She's right. You come from a long line of warriors." Rylan reassured me. "One day, you will see what we all know, what the prophecy has revealed to us." Rylan exhaled, then addressed Jericho and Cairo. "We must meet with all the Wolands who have fought the Carnites. As soon as they land. Stop them." Rylan then turned to face the rest of the council room. "As for the rest of you, you need to rest. We will meet first thing after rounds in the morning. It seems dire times are ahead."

Everyone nodded to Rylan's command. They begin to file out of the council room. I stayed behind with Eva, I wanted to know if my parents back in Texas were alright, and more about the Carnites. Jericho walked over to me. From over my shoulder, he began to press along the screen. On it, a creature made from stone, who was almost as tall as the trees ran through the woods near my house. With slight ease and great strength, he pulled trees from their roots and chucked them at the Woland guards. I wondered how a creature with such a colossal size could go unnoticed. It would surely be all over the news the next day.

"No one will remember a thing tomorrow. The Wolands are not only trained to fight, but to protect all life. It is their job to ensure no human witnesses our dragonic trials. They would have made sure that no human saw anything and if they did, they would use their mahier to cast a spell over the humans, so they would forget." He took the tablet from me. "Your parents are safe. The Carnites were not there for your human parents, they came for the two of you."

I didn't understand. "How would they even know we were going to be there?"

"It seems they know more than we thought. I-"

The Woland guards stormed through the council room doors and interrupted Jericho. It was clear they had arrived back safely. They trudged over to where Eva and I stood. They each lowered to one knee and bowed their heads to us. I looked around the room at the remaining dragons. My gaze stuck on Rylan, who had a proud look on his face. The guards then stood and moved to Rylan and Sila. They bowed their heads again and took their seats at the table.

"I will escort you both to your rooms. It's best to get some sleep, tomorrow will be a big day." Sila said to Eva and me.

I almost wanted to insist I stay and learn about the Carnites, but Sila was right. I was exhausted, and who knew what tomorrow would bring.

Chapter Twelve

Bannggg. Bannggg.

A loud knock at the door woke me abruptly. The only difference from the last time I awoke from an unexpected thud, was the absence of one red-eyed Woland. Mira quickly helped me get ready and five minutes later, we were out the door to pick up Eva and headed to the council room. By the time we entered the council room, it was completely packed and the air was filled with loud, deep discussion. I resumed my seat from last night, and attempted to catch up on the conversation.

"Disappeared? In the middle of the fight? Rylan roared at Jericho. How does that happen?"

"My King, they must be working with another being, one that can wield mahier, or another magical element. We know Carnites do not hold any magic." He pondered for a moment. "It would explain their disappearance. They could have been planning this for the last ten years." Jericho paused. "I'm concerned for how they knew the Prince and the girl were there. Do they know what they are?"

"You speak as if you are sure that they are the Keeper of Dragons." Allas questioned him.

"I've seen with my own eyes that they are. I've felt the energy that radiates off them. Prince Colton is the warrior who will save us, and this girl," Jericho pointed to Eva, "is the golden dragon who will assist him on his journeys. I am convinced they are the Keeper of Dragons." Jericho stated with confidence.

"If you're right, then we are all in danger, dragons and humans alike." Our existence is in a state of imbalance." Allas wiped a puddle of perspiration from her forehead. I looked over to Rylan, who looked to be in a state of disbelief. "What you're saying is, the time of fear is now." Troubled by her own words, Allas peered around the table.

"We hadn't seen movement from a single Carnite in years. For a while, I had thought they were extinct." I could tell Rylan's once assumption had now caused him a great deal of distress. "We must find out who is aiding them, before it's too late." Rylan began to study the room. His eyes met mine.

"Son, good to see you have arrived. As I am sure you've caught up by now, we lost the Carnites last night." He paused and looked over at Jericho. "We are not sure where they went." My heart sunk. I wasn't sure what all this meant for Eva and I. "You will shadow Jericho until we know more. Do not go anywhere without your guards." He turned to the Wolands, "Do not let him out of your sight." He then positioned his eyes on Eva. "Today, you will meet our Keeper of the Book of Aprella. She will verify if you are indeed the dramon of Aprella's prophecy.

Eva nodded. Instantly, Jules came forward and brushed Eva's arm, gesturing her to follow. Eva looked back at me and grinned. "I'll see you soon."

Let's hope. I wondered what would happen if she wasn't the golden dragon. Surely they would let her stay, I mean she could fly, read minds, and a host of other magical talents. She had to be a dragon of some kind. I lifted my eyes and saw a sad smile spread on Sila's face as she listened in to my internal dialogue. I turned away from her gaze and darted my eyes to the door Eva just exited, I wanted to run after her and get her to safety. A hand on my shoulder brought me back to the other people in the room. It was Rylan.

"You need to focus on your training. If you are the warrior from Aprella's prophecy, the lives of every dragon and human are on your shoulders, son." Rylan squeezed my shoulder one last time before he turned his focus on the remaining council. "You all have jobs to do, get to them. And stay alert."

Rylan turned to depart the council room. Sila followed, but stopped to get one last glimpse of me over her shoulder before disappearing down the tunnel. In desperation, I sent a prayer up. As scared as I was about being this grand warrior of all of Ochana, which the entire world depended on, I was more scared of losing Eva.

"Let's go." Jericho commanded, clearly displeased with my train of thought.

I nodded and followed after him, but my mind still raced. What would happen now? How was I supposed to protect everyone? As we strode through Ochana, I looked around at the other dragons, mostly Siens, who had no idea they were in any danger. The dragons laughed and chatted like it was any old day, and any old time, not one fear. They continued on with their usual activities; setting up and running their open-aired market stands, puffing out large flames of fire with their mouths so they could cook meals for each other, flying low in pods as they soaked up the glory and beauty of Ochana. And each of these dragon's lives were in my hands. I needed to get my head on straight.

"Finally," Jericho stated.

It was only one word, but enough to blaze a fire inside me. If this were all true, I had to find strength. I needed to train. I needed to know what I was up against. I turned to Jericho as we walked through town. "What other creatures can wield mahier?

"Only dragons. But there are other creatures that wield different forms of energy. Depending on the creature, each have their own names, but in human terms, I guess you would call it magic." He shook his head in nausea, as if he detested human words for dragonic considerations.

"These creatures, what are they?"

"We need to focus on the others that would help the Carnites. There aren't many, Carnites on their own are easily defeated, and not easy to form an alliance with. But two creatures come to mind, farro and elden. We need to make contact with them. Get a sense for what they're worth-"

We arrived at command, which interjected Jericho's vocal declarations. I thought about the farro and elden. I had never heard of them, ever. I concocted all sorts of images for what they could look like, maybe large brown beasts with razor sharp teeth and monster claws, the kind of evil creature that would haunt a small child's nightmares and make them too frightened to rest their head on a pillow ever again.

At least we knew where to look for these magical imps, but what would happen when we found them?

We entered the glass building right on the edge of Ochana, It was much busier than the last time I was here. Wolands rushed back and forth, mumbling in different levels of pitch, working busy at their tasks, and completely ignoring Jericho and I. We walked straight to Jericho's office. I took a seat in front of his large desk as he pulled a tablet from his side drawer and perused its contents. His eyes widened.

Crack!

Jericho slammed the tablet on his desk so hard it completely shattered from a glowed screen to black bits and pieces. Immediately, Jericho and I looked up as we could we feel someone lurk. Garrik stood in the doorway.

"The farro? Are you sure?" He pierced through Garrik with one of his terrifying looks.

"Looks that way, we've been tracking an increased movement from the Grove. No sign of the

Carnites, but you know how tricky the farro are." Garrik paused to look at me. "Should we attempt contact?"

Jericho began to pace around his office. I focused my attention on him with the hopeful notion that maybe just maybe I could read his mind. There must be more to it than just focus, though maybe not, and it came back to me that I still couldn't open doors, my mahier seemed slow, almost impaired. So far, all I could do was shift into my dragon, and fly. I began to laugh at myself, *all I could do.*

"Do you find this amusing?" Jericho stopped his pacing and sneered at me. "The farros are involved. Those tricky little beasts are too smart for their own good. I'd bet my life they know exactly who you are. Somehow they are two steps ahead of us." He continued to pace. "Two steps ahead," he mouthed to himself, though loud enough for Garrik and I to hear, and ponder for ourselves.

"How? We didn't even know?" Garrik stared at me, brows furrowed in thought.

"We've missed something. We've missed a lot of somethings."

Jericho slammed his hands against one of the glass walls of his office. Like his tablet, I was shocked they didn't shatter. Within an instant, smoke started to billow out from behind his ears and shoulders as he shook in anger. I jumped out of my seat and began to say something, but the words left me.

I stood against the opposite wall in complete astonishment. His eyes glowed as he took in my expression, then he stormed out of his office and into the glass building's main entrance. In a flinch, he shifted into his dragon and took off.

"I haven't seen that in many years." Garrik remarked. "Jericho has been in control for a long time, but your arrival has changed all that." He turned and looked out the glass wall, watching as Jericho soared through the clouds. A line of smoke trailed behind his path.

"How many years?" I was barely able to pay attention to Garrik, I was too focused on Jericho.

When I was met with silence, I looked over at Garrik, who continued to follow Jericho's enraged movements in the sky.

He sighed, "I'd say close to two hundred years."

Was he kidding?

"I remember it like it was yesterday. It was the night councilman Jago died. Jericho was extremely close with him, it came to no surprise when the council voted Jericho in as his successor." A look of sorrow crossed his face. "It's one of the reason Jericho is so serious, he vowed to never let something like that happen again. He's devoted his life to the Woland guard." He turned to Jericho's desk and started to clean up the remains of the broken tablet. "He'll be back soon. I'm surprised he left you at all. I'll be right out that door," he pointed to Jericho's office entrance, the only door in the room. "If you need anything. Two guards will patrol outside the room until Jericho returns."

Garrik bobbed his head and left, leaving me alone. I watched as he summoned two guards and placed them right where he said he would. The two Wolands instantly went into guard mode, ignoring my presence. I sighed and turned back to the glass wall. I could no longer see Jericho, but I hoped he would be back soon, especially after hearing that he had been alive for 200 years! That news astonished me. I wondered how old he was and how old dragons live to?

A loud bang from the command center caught my attention. I walked to the door, but was stopped by two arms spread across the doorway. I looked at the two Woland guards, who shook their heads at me. *I guess I'm not allowed to leave.* I poked my head out to see what the commotion was. I could still hear thuds and all visible Wolands appeared frazzled. *What was going on?*

"Sir, we've lost all communication, in and out." The Woland sounded anxious as he spoke quickly to Garrik. "Everything is black."

"Micah, get ahold of King Rylan and someone find Jericho." Garrik banged on one of the computers, with no luck.

The door swooshed open and Jericho walked in with a look of confusion on his face. He looked right at Garrik. "What in Aprella's name is going on? I was gone five minutes." I sensed aggravation in his voice.

"We've lost communication. We are troubleshooting now." He knocked on the computer again for good measure.

"What do you mean?" Jericho looked around the command center; he noticed all the blank screens and frantic Wolands. "How is this even possible, it's all powered by our mahier?" His brows scrunched as he continued to gaze at the chaos.

"Explain."

I jumped at the sound of Rylan's voice. I hadn't heard or seen him enter. It seemed Jericho and Garrik didn't either. Rylan stood stock still in front of the main doors as he gazed around the room. Everyone froze for a moment as they looked about the black screens of the monitors. Jericho walked to the large glass wall that overlooked the clouds. He searched the sky, for what I didn't know. He turned and addressed the Wolands.

"Everyone, get in your positions. We will know soon what is going on." He turned my way. "My Prince, stand by me." His eyes fumed. "Garrik, release the first realm, set up a perimeter around Ochana."

I raced over to Jericho, for some reason his presence eased my fear a bit. Rylan stepped up beside me. We began to stare out the large glass window, but the sudden chirp from the screens coming alive made me jump. Everyone in the room turned to look at the large screen in the middle of the room. A young white haired woman stared back at us. She looked small, like a pixie. She smiled slowly to reveal sharp pointy teeth. In mere seconds, she went from seemly innocent, to a dwarf-size demon.

"Good morning, dragons." Her raspy voice reverberated from the speakers. "Ah, it seems I am in the presence of royalty. My King, My Prince," The woman sneered as her whole body shook with laughter.

"Who are you and what do you want?" Rylan demanded.

"How rude of me, My King. I am Queen Tana of Farro Grove. I would like to meet with you to discuss an alliance." She was serious.

"We do not give coalition to fallen creatures, like a farro. Now, tell me what you really want."

"Very well. I offer you a trade." Her midnight eyes roamed the room as if she was really able to see everyone in the room, even those out of her peripheral view.

"Continue."

"We will stop the war that has already begun, if you give us the Keeper of Dragons."

"I know nothing of war or the Keeper of Dragons." Rylan spat.

"We must be honest with each other, King Rylan. You met the first wave of our attack just the other night. Those dumb Carnites are just the start. As for your denial of the Keeper of Dragons, I see one half of the pair as we speak. The other half isn't far off, in the Temple of Aprella. I will give you twenty-four hours to decide. Good day, My King." She roared maliciously until the screens cut her off to resume standard function.

"How?" It was the only word Rylan seemed to utter as he monitored the room and looked over the stunned faces of the Wolands.

"Jericho and Garrik punched at the screens. "The Woland guard see's nothing. No one has breached Ochana." Jericho looked back at Rylan.

"That is where you are wrong. That farro broke through our mahier and took control of our communication networks. She had eyes in this very room, and all around Ochana. Find out how she succeeded. Now!" Rylan stormed from the command center, As soon as he entered the outside, he shifted into his dragon, mounted his wings, and took off.

J.A. Culican

Chapter Thirteen

"We need eyes on the Grove." Jericho barked. "Garrik, I want you to lead the mission." He turned from Garrik to face the rest of the Wolands. "Keep realm one on the perimeter, and send guards to the Temple of Aprella. He paused to examine his shattered tablet. Find me a new tablet, and bring me the golden dragon"

Jericho continued to shout out orders around the command center as he stormed from one computer to the next. I watched the Wolands jump at his orders and race to complete his commands. I stayed put. I was still in a state of shock by what had just transpired. The Queen of the farro's had just taken complete control over the communication at Ochana's command center. If we were back home, I wouldn't be too impressed with the hack, but it seems everything here ran off mahier, and only dragons are able to wield it. *Maybe they have a dragon on their side?* A chill ran up my spine as I considered it, would someone really betray their own kind? And for what reason? Or maybe they have learned how to manipulate it somehow? The more I thought about it the more questions I had, and my fear escalated with each one of those thoughts.

"My Prince, it is best that you stay in Jericho's office. It is the safest place in the command center. We need to keep you and-" Garrik trailed off as his eyes wandered to the door. Eva had entered, and was accompanied by two guards. "Ah, the golden dragon has arrived." Garrik beckoned Eva and I over, and led us into the office. He nodded to the guards, who took their spots at the door.

I turned to face Eva. She didn't say a word to me. Her eyes were wide in wonder as she gazed through one of the glass walls. The view was especially breathtaking; a mist of clouds glided slowly through the sapphire sky as the waterfall streamed down from Ochana, making its way all the way down to earth. Eva's wonder made me realize that I hadn't had time to revel enough at the beauty of Ochana, I hail from a land that floated high above the earth, almost like a hot air balloon, while beautiful gleams of purples and turquoises poured from a glorious waterfall. It looked like a liquid milky way with magical powers. And the mountains, the mountains! One of the points was so high it peaked above the haze. I spotted patches of colorful trees and flowers laden along the smoother surfaces of the mountain edges. What a view. What a place to be born. It was hard to believe we were in the middle of, well a war. That was the word Queen Tana had used. We were at war, and didn't even know it. My thoughts then turned to Eva, I wondered what she was told, if they were able to verify who or what she was.

"What did they say to you? I asked hesitantly.

Eva turned her eyes to me, a light gold shined from them. They were no longer the usual bright blue I expected them to be. "Are we really the Keeper of Dragons?"

"Yes, it is true. And there is no need for you to worry about my fate." She gave me a small grin and turned back to our glass view. "Meka had begun to tell me what this all means, but the guards came rushing in." Her body stiffened. "I had no idea what was happening, I still don't."

I didn't know where to start. It took me a few seconds to figure out what I should tell her. I didn't want her to see how scared I was about it all, but before I knew it, I began to explain everything to her, everything about the Queen of the farro's and how she was able to break through the mahier. I nodded towards Jericho, who was still barking orders to anyone in his ear space. "He's been like this since the computers came back on."

Eva watched Jericho as he bounced from one guard to the next. "Has that ever happened before?" Her eyes remained on Jericho.

"I don't think so. Everyone seemed surprised. Rylan was furious. He shifted and took off as soon as we were back online."

Eva turned my way. I could tell she was struggling to say something. "You know, it will be our jobs to take on the farros. I mean we are the Keeper of Dragons. We are fated to save them all, from all enemies." She glanced to the ground then back up to me. "Meka showed me the prophecy. The more time we spend with each other, the stronger our powers will become. I don't think it was a coincidence that I moved next door to you when I was ten. I have a feeling our fate has been laid out for us long before we were born." She paced over to the window and gazed at the clouds in contemplation.

I knew what she said was true, I didn't believe in coincidences. I just wondered what force had brought us together as children, and why. How were we supposed to take on the farros? Let's face it, the farros were not going to wait for Eva and I to complete our training before raging insufferable war on the dragons of Ochana. We would have to figure out a way to defeat them in our lowly dragonic states.

"The Woland guards will back you throughout this journey, and every journey in the future. The farro are only one class of evil that you will face in your life." Jericho explained as he walked into his office. He stood next to Eva and mirrored her stance. Silently, they both gazed out the window as the clouds drifted by.

Even the calming beauty of the scenery could not comfort me. "How many creatures are out there?" Jericho and Eva continued to observe Ochana through the glass.

"The number is endless, you will defeat one, and more will appear. It is the way of the world, especially the life of a protector. The life of being the Keeper of Dragons." Jericho never turned in my direction.

"How will we defeat them? We don't even know what farros are, let alone any of the other creatures." My mind raced on this endless loop of my imminent life.

"You have dragonic support. We will aid you in your fight." Jericho turned to face me. "You have the knowledge of the council at your whim, all you need to do is ask and you will have all that you need." Jericho's head tilted to the side as he scrutinized me. "Your biggest challenge will be with yourself. You feel as though you are not strong enough for the challenges you will face." Jericho sighed, "Time will be your proof." He turned towards Eva, "You have a strong ally in the golden dragon. I can feel the mahier pour from her. You will learn to share the burden with your partner."

He turned and walked back out to the command center. At least he seemed to be back in control. He was right. I had resources at the tip of my claws. All I needed to do is utilize them. Not to mention Eva. I needed to draw from her strength, and lead by her example. Finally, my confidence began to build up. But then...

"My Prince," Garrik bowed his head through Jericho's office doorway. "I need to escort the two of you to the council room. It seems an emergency council meeting has been called. The Keeper of Dragons is needed to discuss our stance with the farro." He gestured for us to follow him.

Eva and I followed Garrik. The two guards at the door followed, with Jericho taking up the rear. I took a moment to internally appreciate Garrik, who always surprised me with his show of respect. I was just a kid he had just met, and yet he bowed to me as if I had proven to him my worth as his Prince.

The walk to the council room had quickly become familiar. Now, it seemed the only two places I could successfully find on Ochana were the command center and the council room, but only as long as I was in one when going to the other. I really needed to find myself a map.

Just as Garrik said, the entire council was in attendance. I took my designated seat next to Rylan. They were recapping the breach from Queen Tana. Disbelief swept the room. Looks of astonishment crept over the faces of each man and woman.

"How is this possible?" Luka questioned. "Farros are powerful, but not as powerful as us."

"The fairies have either evolved in strength and supremacy, or they are getting help from an even more powerful creature."

"Who can be more powerful?" A few dragons murmured in the council.

"Another dragon." Jericho remarked, astounded by his own speculation.

"Dragon?" Rylan bellowed at Jericho. "Impossible! Who would dare aid a sworn enemy of ours, and place their own kind in danger?" His green eyes inflamed as he examined Jericho closely.

Jericho didn't seem bothered by Rylan's fury. "We must investigate all options, my King. If the farros have evolved to this degree, we may have to call in some of our allies."

"Not yet. Let's wait until we get the reports from the second realm." Rylan's glare softened a bit as it shifted my way. "We now have the Keeper of Dragons to help in our fight." He raised his eyebrows at me with a small smirk.

"Indeed, my King," Luka answered. "But they have yet to be trained. We must be hesitant about sending them out to fight just yet..."

Jules interrupted him, "They wouldn't have been sent to us now if they weren't meant to be used in this war. The Prince and the girl are not here by chance. We must utilize them in the means of which they were created to do so."

I sensed that Jules was ready to send us off to war in an instant. At the moment, I found myself thankful for Luka, he understood our lack of skills and our need to train. I looked over to Eva. She was lost in thought, I watched her as she scanned the council. Periodically she would stop and hold one's attention before moving on to the next, until her eyes landed on Allas's. I realized she was sizing them up.

"What about you?" Eva addressed Allas. "You have stayed quiet through this whole exchange. What do you think we should do?" Eva challenged.

Allas exhaled, "Queen Tana says we are at war. If she wants a war, then I say we give her one. Jules is right. These two Keeper of Dragons were sent to us for a reason. I believe this impending war is that reason. We are at the time of great fear, and a battle is to be fought." Allas' green eyes locked with Eva's golden ones. Tension grew amongst the room.

"We will vote," Rylan's declared. "All in favor of sending the Keeper of Dragons out with the Woland guard to the Grove place their insignia in front of the Leslo in Allas' name. All in favor of keeping the Keepers of Dragons here in Ochana to train, place your insignias in front of the Sien in Luka's name."

Rylan and all four councilmen stood. In some kind of ritual, they circled the room and bowed to each founder's image. They then placed their hand on what looked to be the heart of the dragon. He recited a phrase I could not hear. When he removed his hand from the wall, he left a small symbol imprinted on it. The other three councilmen walked to the Leslo and did the same. Once everyone had voted, they returned to their seats.

"The council has spoken. Once the second realm has verified the farros are at the Grove. The Keeper of Dragons will accompany the Woland guard and defeat the threat of war." Rylan nodded in consent and stood. He looked directly at Eva and I, "The lives of all are now in your hands, Keeper of Dragons."

No pressure.

Chapter Fourteen

Word came first thing the next morning. The farros were at the Grove. The second realm had stayed to observe their activity. My guess, the farros knew they were there, but were waiting for Eva and I to arrive. Queen Tana had made it clear who she was after, it was us she wanted. The Queen of the farros saw us as a threat, the ones who could defeat her and her wicked tribe, but I knew what our fate would be if she was successful in capturing us. The question was how do we defeat them?

"You seem so sure the Queen considers us a threat." Eva observed from reading my mind. "She thinks we are the way to defeat all dragons, to use us against our own kind." Eva contemplated.

"It seems she already has a way to defeat us. Look what happened yesterday." I still considered what

Eva said, did Queen Tana really think we would betray our own?

"I think she has a different plan for us." Her voice was strong with conviction.

With our guards in tow, we walked to the command center. As we neared the glass building, I could see the high-story walls beaming as they reflected around Ochana. The beautiful sight did nothing to calm my nerves, though. My anxiety rushed as I pondered what would happen after we entered.

As we arrived at the command center, I could see that a hundred extra guards had been called in. In complete soldier mood, they stood back straight, as their eyes remained un-flinched and staring directly ahead. They didn't move a muscle as we walked past. As Eva and I entered the office, Jericho and Cairo were in a deep conversation, neither of them paused their discussion with our arrival. The two guards left the room to reoccupy their positions at the door. Surprisingly, Jericho seemed calm, in total control.

I had expected the smoke-puffed hothead from yesterday.

Finally, they broke conversation, as Cairo acknowledged us. He gestured to the two chairs near Jericho's desk. We sat in silence as we waited for instruction. Cairo seemed tense, but it was no surprise. The council had voted for two eighteen-year-old, untrained dragons to defeat a race of malicious fairies. I considered the fact that we didn't even know where the farros lived or what they were capable of.

"Ask your questions, I thought I made this clear yesterday." Jericho said grimly. No one expects you to know all the answers when we, who have lived hundreds of years do not."

"How old are you?" *Hundreds of years?*

Jericho chuckled and shook his head. "Well I wasn't expecting a laugh this morning. I am relatively young at around five hundred." Jericho put his hands up to pause my next question. "Before you go any further, each dragon is destined to live a different life; however, most live to be well over a thousand."

That bit of information intrigued me, especially since Rylan had referred to Jericho and the rest of the council as elders when I was first introduced. In reality, Jericho was more middle aged than an actual elder.

"Enough of all that, we need to focus on our mission. Hold your questions about dragons for when you return." He sighed

"How do we defeat the farros?" Eva interrupted.

Jericho nodded his head. "The farros were the first beings to ever challenge a dragon. They have been around since almost the start." Jericho paused and picked up a remote, a large hidden monitor came down from the ceiling. "This..." Jericho played with a remote he grabbed off his desk, "Are the farros."

The monitor came to life with a depiction of what looked to be around a dozen small creatures. Though they mostly had human characteristics, each farro had a head of platinum hair and small silvery flaxen wings that fluttered from their scrawny backs. Sharp, piercing teeth protruded from their thin-lipped mouths, and menacing, pitch black eyes that seemed bottomless. If it weren't for their razor-edged teeth and sinister eyes, they would have looked just like the fairies' children see illustrations of in fairytales. The farros moseyed around a dreadful looking garden that was covered in dead plants, wilted leaves, and broken stems.

"This is the first known picture that we have of the farros. You are right in your thinking. They are directly related to fairies. There is just one main difference," Jericho paused and looked directly at me. "These fairies are The Fallen."

"Fairies?" I asked.

"Fallen?" Eva's query followed mine.

"You are a dragon, you've heard the Carnites, and now you are questioning fairies?" Jericho asked.

His point made me feel ridiculous, I would need to get used to the fact that things I didn't believe existed, actually existed.

"Fairies are innately good; however, a select few weren't happy with their role in creating peace in nature. They wanted more, and so, they allowed their greed to consume them. Back then, all creatures were bonded together as a tight, cohesive unit, and a war amongst us never seemed possible." Jericho shook his head and walked towards the glass wall. "The good fairies banished The Fallen from their home, in belief that they were poisoning their duties."

"The farros searched for a home of their own. They finally landed in Sikkim, India, it's where they have been ever since, where you will be going in just a few hours." Cairo finished Jericho's story.

"How do we defeat them?" Eva asked, I could see as her wheels turned with possibilities.

"It's not that easy. Their mere existence is proof we haven't ever been successful in exterminating them. We thought after our last battle they had finally realized they were over matched. That no matter how many times they tried to stop us we would continue to protect all that was true." Jericho turned from the wall to Eva. "I wish I had a real answer for you. We have been successful in diminishing their numbers, but they are still here, and may never banish for good."

Cairo interrupted Jericho, "Let's focus on our mission. We need to stop this war. Queen Tana said it was only a start with the Carnites. Which means we need to assume they have commandeered other allies." Cairo scrunched his brows in thought. "We need to break up these alliances. Together they may be strong, but apart they know we can overpower them, especially now that we have the Keeper of Dragons."

"Do you know who their other allies are?" Eva asked.

"No. Realm two hasn't seen any other being but the farros at the Grove. Not that I expected it to be that easy. The farros are smart, never underestimate them." Cairo walked to the door and shut it.

"Thank you Cairo." Jericho uttered. "We don't know the role you both are going to play in this mission. Mostly, because we aren't sure what the two of you are capable of. But I agree with the council, you were sent to us for a reason, and I believe this was it." He stated with confidence. "Now, you will be guarded at all times by realm five of the Woland guard. Realm five consists of five highly trained Wolands. They will protect you with their lives. They have already been briefed. They understand the Keeper of Dragons is what the farros want and that we believe the two of you are the only ones who can end this." Jericho stated.

"We will leave soon, setting us to arrive at nightfall. The farros gave us twenty-four hours to hand the two of you over. Cairo walked towards the door. "Pull yourselves together, let's go meet realm five."

We walked through the doorway back into the command center. I expected a flurry of activity, but everyone was calm, like today was any other day. The guards looked like they hadn't moved an inch since we last saw them. I was impressed with their discipline. We stopped in front of five imposing Wolands. They towered over Jericho and Cairo, each one held a similar scowl on their face, red eyes burned in my direction.

"Wolands were created for battle, My Prince. Warriors." Cairo looked at me over his shoulder. "These men here are realm five."

Each Woland looked in my direction and bowed in respect. I always felt uncomfortable when one showed their respect to me, more so now. These men deserved my respect not the other way around. I could tell just by the look of them that these Woland had been to war many times and had been victorious.

"It's an honor to meet you all." Eva's strong voice carried to the Wolands, their attention shifted to her.

"The Keeper of Dragons, we devote our lives to you. It is an honor to go to battle with you. Our lives are in your hands now." The largest Woland of the group addressed us.

"This is Jude, High Guard of realm five. He will be in charge of your safety. You both do as he says." Jericho looked right at Eva as he spoke.

I wondered why he pegged Eva as the troublemaker, or maybe he just pegged me as the scaredy cat too terrified to step a toe out of line, which I was. Eva always challenged authority, not in a disrespectful way, more in a knowledgeable way. She was quick, able to survey and make sound decisions with little problem. She was going to make the perfect golden dragon for Ochana.

"Let's move out. As soon as we land in Sikkim take your positions. Everyone keep your senses open and be prepared. The farros know we're coming." Jericho took off toward the door, the Woland guard followed close behind.

Eva and I trailed behind them with realm five. I watched as all the Woland began to shift, Eva elbowed me and gestured for me to follow suit. I inhaled a large breath and began my shift. I couldn't wait for my shifts to become as fluid as everyone else's. By the time I finished my shift to my dragon, I looked up to see that the Wolands and Eva had lifted into the air already. Their wings flapped as they gawked at me to catch up.

I exhaled and pushed off the ground. As I ascended into the aquamarine sky, realm five encircled Eva and I. They were to border us for the entire flight. The sight truly amazed me, a hundred or so Wolands flew through the sky, their red scales shone through the clouds. I prayed everyone's mahier was strong, I couldn't imagine what a human would think of this sight. That thought made me think of the farros. They proved to us that they could control our mahier once, what would happen when we arrived? Would they be able to control it then to?

Eva's voice floated through my head, "Stay alert. I have a bad feeling. Something feels off."

"What do you mean?" I projected.

"They know we're coming. It feels like a trap."

I laughed at that, of course it was a trap. We had no idea what we would find when we arrived in India. We didn't even know who the farros had convinced to help them with this war, besides the Carnite's. Not to mention we had no idea what they wanted with Eva and I.

My pulse raced, tonight would cement our fate.

Chapter Fifteen

I was exhausted. My wings were sturdy and kept me afloat, but all I wanted was to curl up in a ball to go to sleep. As we whipped through a thick cloud, one of the Wolands in realm five turned to Eva and I. He pointed down toward the earth with his claw and made a huffing noise with his fire-breather, which signaled the other Wolands to descend. In synchronicity, we lowered slowly, and, as the clouds parted, a land of green pastures emerged beneath us. Horned beasts roamed on all fours, some were chomping on grass from the ground, and others were lying on it. As we got closer, I realized they were elk. Suddenly, one of the Wolands sent a gust of fire directly into the beating heart of an elk standing as he munched on a plant. It let out a loud cry as it jolted to its demise and all four of its legs collapsed. Alarmed, I looked to Eva, who giggled. The Wolands had caught us dinner.

We set up a picnic along the green field, though Eva had turned her nose up at the thought of consuming raw meat. One of the guards reached for a large branch of a nearby tree, huffed a fire through it, and began to cook a piece of meat for Eva. The guards sure knew how to accommodate us.

After dinner, we rose back into the air to finish our trip to India. Luckily, my portion of elk endowed me with enough energy to finish the journey.

We hauled a little bit longer, until one of the five realm Wolands motioned again for us to descend down to earth. The clouds parted once more, and a few pieces of mounted land appeared. I saw small patches of green land, miniscule trees, and a charming lake. Each dragon started to land, with mine being surprisingly smooth. A faint thud was all that could be heard. Satisfied with my landing, I looked around to see that the other dragons were shifting back into their human forms. It would make our trip around the lake a bit easier.

Jude had explained to us the importance of Mitra Lake in Sikkim. We had to walk around it in order for the Grove to appear. The farros had a magical element they wielded called tillium, it was similar to mahier, but less potent. They had used it to protect their home and shield it from humans. At the end of the trek the farros would lift the shield and allow us entrance, if they chose to.

"How was realm two able to see the Grove? I mean we figured the farros knew they were there, but it shouldn't have been a question if they had to lift their shields to allow entrance." Eva voiced the thought that had just fluttered through my head.

"Our mahier is much stronger, we are able to see through their shield. We are unaware if the farro know of this, hence our nature walk now." Jude replied.

"Can you see them now, through their shield?" I asked.

"No, my focus is keeping the two of you safe. Other Woland in other realms are tasked with keeping an eye on the farro's activity." He stated as he maneuvered over a large boulder.

If it weren't for the battle we had flown all this way for, I would have been in awe of the scenery. We were in Northern Sikkim, the population here was very low, almost nonexistent at our exact location. We walked along the shore of a mighty lake in a valley between mountains. The mountain peaks were frozen and I could see snow scattered about. The lake was calm, but seemed to be free of any wildlife. Either they could feel the presence of dragons and fled or this was part of the allure. Boulders and rocks were scattered about the shore, which made our trip difficult as we stepped over rocks and dodged the uneven surfaces. I had to give it to the farros, they were smart, any enemy of theirs who wished to meet with them would be exhausted by the time the shield was lowered. Not to mention it gave them time to prepare. Speaking of which, I could already feel the eyes of the farros on us. They knew we were here. I wondered if we could drop their shield and catch them off guard.

"Can our mahier lower their shield?" I asked Jude in a tentative voice, I was no soldier so strategy was not something I excelled in.

"We have never tried. Again we do not want the farros to know the extent of our abilities. Even if we could, our goal is to stop a war, not initiate one. We will attempt a diplomatic solution before we progress to war."

"But they attacked us, twice. War has already started." I objected

"That was not war, those were battles. We have had great wars in the past, many creatures and humans lost their lives. It is not something we want to repeat. Unfortunately, creatures like the farros do not care about the wellbeing of humans or even the loss of their own kind. They only care about one thing."

"What's that?"

"Power. To be at the top of the food chain." Jude explained.

"Then what? I mean if they ever got there?" I asked as my voice started to shake.

"My guess, they would fight each other until only one remained. Creatures like the farros are selfish. Yes, they'll work together, now. But once they've won, they will fight each other in order to have complete control and power over the entire kinship." Jude expounded.

"But nothing will be left." I whispered.

"That is why we have been tasked with the job as protectors. We protect all that is true from beings like the farros. So nothing like that will ever happen"

"I'm starting to understand just how important the dragons are." Even if the idea terrified me.

"Ah, and you haven't even seen everything." Jude locked eyes with me. "When you do, you must stay strong. We all need you."

***

We made it around a good portion of the lake when the ground began to shake. Everyone stopped to look around. I could see the snowcaps on the mountains start to move and slide down the mountainsides. The Wolands threw their hands up in an attempt to stop the snow with their mahier, but the snow continued as if the dragons had done nothing.

"Shift, get into the air." Jude commanded of realm five.

"I can't"

"Something's wrong."

"My mahier..."

No matter what we tried, none of us could shift. The Wolands looked around lost. They didn't know what to do without their mahier. I grabbed Eva's hand and started to run into the lake. We braced ourselves as we dived in. The water felt like ice, but if we remained on dry land, the avalanche would sweep us away. The Wolands noticed our escape, and followed. We swam out as far as we could, my teeth chattered and my body shivered. I watched as the snow barreled down the mountainside towards us. Right when it was about to hit the edge of the water, it disappeared.

Suddenly, we were no longer in the water, or even in the valley. All hundred or so of us dragons seemed to have transported to a remote region. A moment ago, we were in one of the most beautiful scenic areas I had ever seen, but now, we stood in what looked to be a frozen tundra. The ice-cold temperature distressed me. I held on to Eva's hand as realm five closed in around us, I searched for any clue as to what happened. I looked up to the sky and saw the farros peppering the sky.

"Welcome." Queen Tana's voice echoed around the open space. "To Farro Grove." Her arms went wide in welcome.

I wasn't feeling very welcomed. I felt trapped. Scared. No one moved or replied to the Queen. Every Woland stood in attack mode; ready for the fight I was sure to come. I gripped Eva's hand tighter, she turned in my direction, and I could see it. Scales began to cover her face, she held her finger up to her mouth for me to be quiet, then tilted her head towards the farros above us.

"I see you found our entrance without a problem." Tana clapped her hands. "Bravo! I'm hoping you brought my old friends with you?" She inquired as she gazed around the Wolands.

Tana stopped at Eva and me with a fear induced smile that showed off her razor sharp teeth. "Ah, come here my Keeper of Dragons, I have missed you so." With a wave of her hands Eva and I started to levitate off the ground. Jude and the other Wolands attempted to grab onto us and pull us back, but their effort was useless. The farros circled around them and released silver sparks at the realm five Wolands until they fell to the ground. Queen Tana floated over to us and examined our features with her midnight eyes. She reached out to touch the scales on Eva's face, but Eva swatted her hand away.

"I have to thank you two. You have kept myself and the rest of the farros quite entertained the last eight years. You have given us much time to prepare for today. It is time to officially adopt you into our tribe."

"Were not interested in joining you or your tribe." Eva shouted at her.

Tana chuckled, "You my dear are just like me. Beautiful. Strong. Cunning. Fearless. You belong with us. Together we can rule all." Tana smirked at us and turned to the Woland. "You all look confused. Shall I tell you a story?"

I searched the crowd for Jericho and Cairo, I knew they were there somewhere. It was hard to see the faces of the Woland, the sky was dark with only a few visible stars. The farros zipped around us in an excited frenzy. I began to make out the Wolands from the other side of Queen Tana but I couldn't be sure. I attempted to angle my head to get a better view, but Queen Tana broke my search.

"Pay attention, Coley," Tana mocked. "This is important."

How did she know about my mom's nickname for me? No one but her ever called me that, and she never called me it in front of anyone. Almost like she knew I wouldn't be able to live down that embarrassment.

"We found you when the two of you were young. We were drawn to the energy that surrounds you, we have watched you grow through the years. At first we had no idea what it meant or who you were. We spent the first few years searching for answers. Until we found it. You were the Keeper of Dragons, and we the farros were the only ones who knew. Not even the dragons or that arrogant King Rylan knew." Tana sneered as she spoke of Rylan the King.

"How did you know? We didn't even know." Eva questioned.

"Answer this my girl, when is the last time you were sick? Broke a bone? Needed stitches?" Tana just shook her head at us. "It was obvious something was special about the two of you. You fed off each other's energy. An energy that shined to us like a beacon in the sky, the day you met, we felt it."

"Enough. Do you honestly think we are going to let you take the Keeper of Dragons from us?" Jericho voiced from below us.

"What do you think you can do about it, dragon? I'm sure you've noticed your mahier is of no good here. As I said, we have been preparing for this day for many years." Tana snickered. "Today shall be your last." She commanded.

"How?" I choked out.

"How what, my boy?" Tana mocked.

"How did you take our mahier?" I was confused.

"Did you think we would be unprepared to take on the mahier? Without it, dragons are nothing but human. It's ironic, really. Dragons have devoted their lives to protect humans, and other fragile creatures. But today they will meet their end, just like a human."

The farros started to laugh. It sounded more like a hive of angry bees preparing to strike. I looked over at Eva. We had to do something. The Wolands counted on us, we were the Keeper of Dragons after all. If we were defeated tonight, it would be the end of all dragons.

"Oh, I almost forgot. I have a surprise for you, a little family reunion. You asked how, this may give you the answer you desire." Queen Tana leered at us.

She nodded to a group of farros, who took off behind a large boulder. The boulder split open, and a figure started to appear. I squinted my eyes to get an unblemished view. Immediately, I could tell this was no farro, this was much larger than a farro.

It was Zane.

J.A. Culican

Chapter Sixteen

I couldn't take my eyes off him. The rest of the dragons back in Ochana were displeased with Zane, and a little worried about him, but this? Would he really betray us all? And if so, why?

"How's it hanging, nephew of mine?" Zane chuckled as he walked closer to us. "Tana, let them down, I'd like to see my nephew's eyes as he learns the truth."

"Why?" Was all I could choke out as Tana released me and I tumbled to the ground.

"The Grove is all yours, Zane." Tana swung her arms around, "And look, you have the full attention of the Woland guard. I'm always up for a story!" Queen Tana chimed in.

Zane looked around at each Woland, his eyes stopped on Jericho and Cairo. "Ah look, you brought some of my closest friends, thank you Colton." He laughed as he turned back towards me.

"These dragons are your family, and Cole is your nephew. Why would you do this?" Eva questioned.

"The golden dragon, it is an honor to be formally introduced." He put his hand out to shake Eva's

She glared at his outstretched hand. "Like I would shake the hand of the enemy." She sneered.

"You were right about her Tana, I like her." He laughed. "However, let's get back to why we're here." He turned back to me. "You've already heard the story about my big brother Jago, what you don't know is what happened after. Answer me this, Prince Colton. Have you had the honor to meet your grandparents yet?"

I thought about the question, my grandparents had never been mentioned, I just assumed they had passed. "No, I didn't know they were still alive." I replied.

"Oh they are most definitely alive, banished from Ochana for the death of their son." Spittle flew from his mouth as he sneered out those words. "And of course, being the dutiful son that Rylan was, agreed to this punishment as his first ever ruling as King." Zane stressed the words to drive his point home.

"Liar!" Cairo shouted. "How could you?"

Jericho placed his hand on Cairo's shoulder to calm him down while his eyes never left Zane. He said nothing. A look I didn't understand passed between them. Jericho stood tall and lifted his chin. His eyes shifted to mine and nodded his head, it happened so fast I wondered if I had imagined it.

"Revenge or jealousy? Which is the real reason you betrayed your race?" Eva asked.

Zane shook his head at her, "Don't you see? I'm justified in my actions. The dragons turned their back on their own race. Scared creatures that they are."

"Which we gladly used to our advantage." Queen Tana interjected. "Zane here has been helping us gain control of your mahier for years, the Keeper of Dragons couldn't have come at a better time, for we control your mahier, which means we control you!" She proclaimed with a sneer.

"Actually, I control the mahier." Zane clarified. "See the farros gave me the use of their tillium and together with how potent my own mahier is, I was able to manipulate your mahier any way I wanted." Zane declared.

"Now that you have it, what's your plan?" Eva questioned.

"Lucky for you, you haven't been around long enough to form any true friendships." Tana replied with venom.

"First, another story." Zane interrupted. "This one is my favorite. It's a new story just for the farros. Gather around." He gestured with his hands for the farro to join him. The other fallen fairies scampered around Zane as they squeaked out high-pitched snickers.

"Make it quick Zane, I am getting antsy!" Tana requested.

"Of course." He looked over to her and smirked. "Jago and I were very close before his death. I often accompanied him on his rounds, as a way to understand the Wolands, for I was trained as a Leslo."

"That experience has aided us on our journey." Tana added.

"I agree." He cleared his voice. "I was with him during his final round. We were circling Ochana, checking the perimeter."

"What?" Tana interrupted.

Zane put up his hands to stop her from questioning him. "We saw something stuck on the ice, we thought it was an animal of sorts. As we flew closer, we noticed it was a boat, but humans hardly came that far north, and when they did it was because something was wrong. Being a protector, Jago flew over to the boat, hoping he could save the humans aboard. He took off ahead of me, and by the time I got to him, it was too late." Zane looked to the ground, his pain was evident.

"I don't understand." I whispered. None of this made sense.

Zane looked up and pierced me with a look. "He was attacked. The boat wasn't full of humans like he thought. It was a trick. The boat was full of farros." Zane looked to Tana with an odd expression on his face.

"That's ridiculous. You lie?" Tana shouted.

"Jago was the strongest warrior of all the Wolands. Did you honestly think an attack with just the use of your tillium would leave him for dead so quick?" He shouted back. "He told me what happened, made me promise him that I would find the farros, and end them." He sneered.

Zane bent back and shifted into his dragon. Instantly, fire flew from his mouth and his mammoth claws thumped along the ground, right where the farros had gathered. They scuttled around in madness; some fluttered off the ground, others dashed toward the mountains. I felt my mahier creep back through my fingertips. I turned to the Wolands; their mahiers were returning too. Eva grabbed my hand and squeezed. I looked over in time to see her scales shelter her skin. I looked around in fear; the farros and Wolands were in a fight to the death. Eva's squeeze of my hand reminded me that she was still with me, and it was time to fight.

"We can end this. It's why we're here." Eva whispered for my ears only.

"How? Look around, we're standing in the middle of a war."

"Grab my other hand and hold on tight. Focus all your energy on the farros."

"Why? What will that do?" I questioned.

"Use your instincts. I am."

I lowered my head and rested it on Eva's forehead; her eyes fluttered shut, mine followed. I blocked out the fight that raged around us and focused all my energy on the farros. All I could feel were Eva's hands clasped with mine, and her soft breath every time she exhaled, I felt and heard nothing else. My focus was completely on the farros. A vibration started at my toes, it crept through until my entire body pulsed with a new energy. A light shot from the tips of my fingers and separated into tiny strings. Each string attached itself to a farro. By now, each fairy had taken flight and was suspended in air. I yanked my hands back, pulling the tillium out of each farro. When the tillium was completely sucked out, the strings released, and, quite amused, I watched as each farro dropped to the ground.

When the light went out, my body began to tremor. My breaths became strenuous. My body hit the ground hard as the tremors continued. I could hear Eva saying my name, the panic evident in her voice. Moments later the quakes stopped, I could finally take a breath. I opened my eyes to see Eva as she gazed down at me with a look of terror.

"Cole, what happened? Are you alright?" She stammered.

I attempted to sit, "I... don't know what just happened." I said with confusion.

As I looked around, I noticed all the Wolands had shifted back into their human forms, and most of the farros were rigid on the ground. Even as humans, the Wolands towered over the farros. They looked different, but I couldn't quite figure out what it was that made them appear dissimilar to their previous characteristics.

Jericho and Cairo had Queen Tana cornered between them. They looked ready to stomp her out. She turned to me.

"What did you do to me? Just wait until my tillium returns!" She shouted.

"Awful courageous words for someone in your position Tana. I do wonder what your fate will be." Jericho stated with a smirk. He looked my way, "My Prince, are you okay?"

"Yea, I think so." I answered, as I took stock of how I felt. I had an increased amount of energy zipping through my body, it was different than the mahier I was used to when I shifted into my dragon. I had no idea what it was.

"It's tillium." Zane answered my thoughts. "You stole all the farro's tillium with that little trick you just did, it now lives in you. You are very powerful, more so than I gave you credit for." Zane finished with what sounded like pride.

"Give it back, it's not yours to take. You're breaking the rules of our treaty! Tana roared.

"You broke that treaty the night you killed my brother. It has taken me over two hundred years to fulfill my brother's promise. It seems bittersweet that the new Prince of Ochana was the one who defeated you. It is how Jago would have liked it." Zane turned to me. "It has cemented your right as the Prince, Keeper of Dragons." Zane bowed to me, the rest of the Wolands followed.

"What about the rest?" Eva pointed to the farros. "What are we supposed to do with them?"

It was a good point. Even without their tillium we couldn't leave them here. They could always figure out how to get more or recreate it or, worse, come up with something stronger. And they couldn't come back to Ochana with us. I looked over to Jericho and Cairo for an answer. Neither said a word.

"The decision is Prince Colton's." Zane answered. "He speaks for the King when the King is not present."

"Me? Why not you, you are also a Prince." I asked.

"You rank higher than me, you are the King's successor. Not to mention the Keeper of Dragons." Zane explained. "And let's be honest, not many dragons trust me these days." He winced.

"Zane is right My Prince, the choice is yours." Jericho stated. "As for you," he looked to Zane. "You have earned quite a bit of trust back; however, you will have a lot of explaining to do when we get back to Ochana." He stated sternly.

I felt a hand in mine and turned to see Eva. In silence, she squeezed my hand to show her support in whatever choice I made. I turned towards the

Woland, all of their attention was on me, awaiting a decision. I was about to ask for suggestions when I noticed what looked like a herd of butterflies in the horizon. I squinted as I tried to make out what was there. The Woland turned around and followed my line of sight.

"Is that..."

"The fairies." Zane finished Jericho's thought.

Fairies, I prayed they were nothing like the farros. None of the Woland moved or shifted into their dragons. I took that as a sign of comfort, maybe they were here to help? As the fairies came closer I noticed the similarities between them and the farros. Their size was the same, and so was the stiff platinum hair and spastic silvery wings. Now that I thought about it, that's what was different about the farros. Their wings weren't flapping around in rage; however, that is where the similarities ended. The fairies' eyes were full and bright, each a different neon color, and their smiles flaunted straight teeth and dimples. The fairies landed with gentle grace around us.

"My Prince," the fairy bowed. "I am Queen Annabelle, Queen of the fairies."

"Annabelle, you have perfect timing." Zane acknowledged.

"I see that. I pray none of your dragons were hurt?" She questioned.

"No, my highness, all are fine." Zane smiled towards Annabelle.

"What is your plan with the farros?" She inquired as she gaped at Tana.

"We haven't decided yet." I responded. "They cannot come back to Ochana with us and I don't feel comfortable leaving them

"I see. May I offer a suggestion, Prince Colton?" She asked.

"Of course."

"It is more of a request, truly." Her round eyes widened as she spoke. The farros are ancestors of the fairies. Over the years, we have tried many times to stop the hateful transgressions they have committed. Unfortunately, we have been unsuccessful. I ask that you give the farros over to us, so we can make right on our name and end the farros for good."

I thought about what she requested. If I handed over the farros to the fairies it would solve the problem, and I wouldn't need to make any further decisions on the matter. Even with all their wrongdoings, I felt I couldn't be responsible in deciding their fate, not with the little knowledge I had. And technically, the farros were the fairies' responsibility; they were the ones who expelled them in the beginning. I looked to Eva and she nodded with my decision.

"I grant your request, Queen Annabelle. The farros are your responsibility, and I will put their fate in your hands." I nodded towards the farros.

"Thank you, Prince Colton, Keeper of Dragons." She bowed her head and made a hand gesture to the other fairies. "We will take them back to our home, I will send word to King Rylan when a judgment has been made for their fate."

I nodded in consent as I watched the fairies grab on to the farros with invisible ropes, which seemed to come from their fingers. The farros flailed their scrawny bodies around and shouted to no avail. Tana looked furious as Queen Annabelle grabbed hold of her and flew off. Once the fairies were out of sight, I turned back to the dragons.

"Now what?" I asked.

"Now we go home My Prince, you have a coronation to attend." Zane replied as he shifted into his dragon.

J.A. Culican

Chapter Seventeen

Hours later, we arrived at Ochana. My first inbound glimpse of the magical kingdom was the stunning waterfall, which greeted us with luminous charm as we soared in. I managed to land gracefully in the center of Ochana, the castle lay to my right while the mountains peaked straight ahead. Quickly, dragons from every direction headed over to welcome us back. Some dragons flew in, while others had waited nearby for our entry. The trip home was uneventful; no one spoke much on the way, completely lost in thought about what we witnessed. The biggest surprise of the night had been my Uncle Zane. I was full of curiosity and anticipation for the story he would have to tell soon. My uncle had waited two hundred years for the events that happened mere hours ago to finally unfold.

Rylan and Sila were front and center as I landed. They both rushed over to me. Sila enveloped me in a hug; something I hadn't expected from her, while Rylan gave me a firm pat on the back; a huge beam spread across his face. He walked over to Zane and Jericho while Sila stuck around to greet Eva.

"I am eager to hear everything that happened with Queen Tana and the farros. Come let's gather in the council room. We will have time to celebrate later!" Rylan exclaimed.

Along with the council and a few extra dragons, we began to follow Rylan to the council room. We stepped through the waterfall, and, for the first time since arriving at Ochana, I allowed my senses to enjoy my surroundings; I marveled at the flowing waterfall, and the blue, now cloudless sky that lay overhead. As we stepped into the council room, I realized it looked exactly the same as it did last time I was here, the night the council voted for the destiny of Eva and me. It seemed like so long ago, but in fact it was only last night. I took my assigned seat and waited as everyone shuffled in and got comfortable.

I waited with bated breath to hear the story Zane was about to share.

"Everyone find a seat, we have much to discuss." Rylan turned to Zane. "Let's start from the beginning. The floor is yours brother."

Zane nodded and stood, he started to pace from one end of the room to the other. He fought to find the words to start, he looked up from the ground and his eyes began to wander around the room. Finally, he took a deep breath, and exhaled.

"It all began the night of Jago's death." His eyes stopped on Rylan's. "He was murdered, by the farros."

"How do you know this? The healers they said his mahier was drained?" Rylan sounded skeptical.

"It was. The farros used their tillium to do exactly that. They wanted us to think we were being punished. They used our absence to the outside world to their advantage." Zane pulled at his hair. "They hadn't expected a Woland as strong as Jago, it was dumb luck for the farros to be able to get their hands on the Prince, alone." He paused, "I was with him, but I was too slow to keep up. If he had waited just a few seconds for me..." He trailed off as he looked back to the ground.

"You'd be dead as well." Jericho stated. "The farros would have gotten their hands on two Princes and we would have been none the wiser."

"Why didn't he call for backup when he saw the farros?" Rylan asked.

"He didn't know. We saw a boat out in the sea. We figured some humans were lost or hurt. You knew Jago." Zane shook his head. "He would give his life for the humans. He didn't even stop to question it, just flew off to help them." Zane looked back up. "By the time I got there, the farros were gone and Jago was barely alive."

"Why didn't you tell us all this the night it happened? So much would have been different." Rylan interrupted as he glared at Zane.

"Jago, he made me promise. He didn't want the farros to know he had survived for even a second. If either of us had told you that night, you would have declared war and flown off to battle." Zane glared right back at Rylan. "Right?"

"Of course I'd have. It would have been the right decision."

"No. Jago knew we'd been ignoring our duties as protectors. He wanted his death to mean something, something more than war. He wanted us to remember who we were." He pointed to himself as his voice started to rise, "We are dragons, protectors of all that is true." He paused to let his words sink in to all that were listening. "We had forgotten our responsibilities, our obligations to all. He knew what was happening to him and he knew the conclusion our healers would come to."

"It's been two hundred years Zane." Rylan shouted. "Look at the sacrifices our dragons have made." His arms went wide. "All over a lie."

"He was right, it was the only way. If we'd been doing our jobs we would have seen the farros coming a mile away. Instead we were living in our bubble, ignoring all that was going wrong with the world. Think of all the tragedies we could have prevented." He shook his head and sat back in his chair.

"What happened next? After his death you kept your distance from everyone. You were seen leaving Ochana at odd hours? There were many rumors." Rylan asked.

"I started forming relationships with many ill-fated creatures. My goal was to befriend the farros, and convince them I wanted to destroy the dragons as vengeance for the way I was being treated." He laughed, "It was easy to come up with a plausible story. And of course they bought it. It took many years, but eventually I was brought into their inner fold, let in on many secrets." He turned to Jericho, "You need to get the Woland guard ready. The farros were able to create many allies. Once these creatures get wind of the farros fate, they will come after us and fight in their place."

"Wait." Rylan interrupted. "Why did it take so long? You must have been given many opportunities to end them."

"I did. But one thing led to another. The information they were able to get their hands on was staggering. Every time a situation arose where I could finish them, something would happen. A different creature would approach them, asking to help them in their war. Creatures I thought long extinct were coming out of the woodworks."

"The Carnites?" Rylan asked.

"Were only one of many. We had our guard down for too long, it gave them time to hide, find new homes and make new friends." Zane exhaled loudly before he continued. "We are sitting in the middle of a war. A war none of you knew was even going on."

"Must not be much of a war if we know nothing of it." Rylan stated.

"That's because the war is against you. How many years before Jago's death did we keep our heads in the sand?" Zane asked. "Around a hundred. A hundred years these creatures were building an army, an army to defeat us. The farros may have started it all, but they had just a small part in the grand scheme."

"Where were these creatures tonight? The farro knew we were coming?" Jericho asked. "Their army should've been raring to go."

"Some were there, the Carnites and the eldens." He ticked them off his fingers as gasps went off around the table. "Remember the farros weren't expecting me to turn on them." He paused. "My guess, they saw what our Keeper of Dragons did to the farros and took off."

"Eldens? Are you sure?" Jules whispered, clearly startled by the news.

"Positive. I spoke with King Eldrick myself. They are very much involved in this war." Zane affirmed.

"What happened to the farros?" Rylan asked. "How were you able to defeat them?" He turned my way with an expectant look.

"I don't really know. Somehow I was able to steal their tillium from them." I looked over to Eva, she gestured for me to continue. "I can still feel it running through my body."

"With your mahier?" Rylan asked.

"I don't know." I mean I haven't even mastered opening doors. But somehow I was able to suck all the tillium out of the farros.

"I've tried many times to do what Prince Colton did. I was unsuccessful every time. Even when the farros transferred some of their tillium to me I wasn't able to do much with it. All it did was make my mahier stronger." Zane added.

"I would bet it has something to do with the pair of them." Allas pointed to Eva and I. "Being the Keeper of Dragons and all. There is much we don't understand about them. I will have to speak to Meka again, see if the prophecy says anything about their powers."

"They are another reason my plans were put off." Zane nodded towards us. "Somehow the farros figured out who they were. Tana attempted to explain it to me; she said they were drawn to them, the power within them. She had a constant watch on them for the last eight years. The farros were waiting until they fully came into their powers, then they planned on turning the Prince and golden dragon against you to aid them in their war." Zane explained.

"That would've never happened. We would have never trusted them." Eva stated with conviction.

"Dark creatures have a way with persuasion." Sila added quietly.

"The sun has already rose, you must all get some sleep. Rest and relax, it sounds like we won't have much time in the future for either." Rylan gestured for everyone to stand.

A few murmurs sounded in the council room as everyone filed out. Eva and I waited by the door for Rylan and Sila. My mind raced with the future. More creatures were coming our way, all with the same goal. Defeat the dragons and take control.

"We'll figure it out." Eva stated. "We were able to defeat the farros, I have confidence we will be successful again."

"I'm glad you have so much faith in us. Maybe it was dumb luck? We had no idea what we were doing." I stammered.

"You will train." Jericho interrupted. "We have a program for all new dragons when they return to Ochana. Of course they are usually placed in one course based on their founder. Seeing how you take after all four, we'll have to combine the four courses just for you." He paused, "Well the two of you."

Rylan and Sila walked up beside Jericho, the five of us turned and walked towards the caves that would lead us to the castle. There was one question that still bothered me. Zane had told a story about my grandparents to the farros, it couldn't be true, could it?

"What story is that, my son?" Sila asked.

I turned to Rylan, who stood in close proximity to Sila. "Zane said you banished them from Ochana after the death of Jago. That it was your first ruling as King." I explained.

Rylan chuckled, "Part of that story is true. I did take over as King after Jago's death. But as for your grandparents, they are still here, in Ochana. I believe the human term is retired. After Jago's death, your grandfather stepped down. He held immense guilt for his death."

"Wait, Zane also said something about a coronation, which I needed to get back to Ochana for. You're not stepping down, are you?" There was no way I was ready to be King, Rylan could retire in say five hundred years, I might be ready then. Maybe.

"No, son. But we will be holding a coronation for you, in two days' time. You will be the first Prince to have one. It will be your formal introduction to the dragons here on Ochana." He paused as we stepped into the castle. "The preparations for your return have been going on for a few years now. I expect it will be one of the grandest events ever to be held here."

"Eva darling, come with me I will show you to your room." Sila gestured for Eva to follow her. "Goodnight son, get some rest." Sila squeezed my hand as she walked by and Eva gave me a small wave over her shoulder.

"I'm very proud of you son. Your actions tonight prove you are the true Prince of Ochana. I see great things in your future. Goodnight." Rylan nodded to me and I heard him walk down the hall and chuckle.

I turned and faced my door. I began to laugh loudly. Now was as good a time as ever to practice opening the door.

J.A. Culican

Chapter Eighteen

I woke up to the sun shining in my eyes through the open curtains in my room. It was the day of my coronation, or my royal debut, as I'd rather have it called. I stretched and looked to my door, my new door was closed. It seems my mahier with the added tillium is much stronger than anyone had anticipated. Yesterday morning when I tried to open my door, it completely exploded and turned to dust, which set off every alarm on the island to my complete embarrassment. Once everyone settled and had a good laugh at my expense, I was finally able to get some rest.

Jericho had woken me up later that day to show me the Woland training facilities and explained to Eva and I the different courses on combat and strategy we would be expected to take. He explained to me how the other Woland would test us and make us prove our worth, not just because I was the prince, because Eva and I were the Keeper of Dragons. Jericho then passed us on to Jules, who took us up to the Temple of Aprella. Even though Galians were known as the nurturers, she explained that most of our Galian training would take place here. We were to study the Book of Aprella and learn the long history of the dragons.

Luka had met us on the steps of the Temple to take us into town. It was our first visit into Ochana. Eva and I were in awe at the sights around us. The energy that surrounded the dragons as they bustled about to complete their tasks was intoxicating. While we watched the dragons, Luka explained that we would not complete the same type of course work as the other Siens due to our role as part of the council. Each Sien is trained to complete a specific job, including production of goods or a service provider; each Sien is assessed when they come to age as to what path they will take. Eva and I will be required to take a crash course in both as we shadow different Siens as they complete their tasks and responsibilities, as a way for us to understand the importance of the Sien's work.

Luka then dropped us off in the council room where we met with Allas. She of course deemed the coursework we were to complete with her the most important; leadership and etiquette. Only a small number of dragons ever got the chance to work alongside the Leslos, for their numbers are much lower than the other founding groups.

A knock at the door brought me out of my memories from the day before. I walked over to the door, and with a small chuckle I opened it. I had practiced opening and closing my new door at least a hundred times before I went to bed the night before. Sila's smile greeted me from the other side.

"May I come in son?" She asked with an even bigger smile.

"Of course." I waved her in.

She walked in and had a seat at the table I had only used so far to eat breakfast on. That thought made my stomach growl and wonder where Mira was.

"She is busy helping the others get ready for today. Do not worry, I will escort you to the hall for breakfast." She gestured for me to have a seat next to her. "How are you feeling today? Did you rest well?"

"I did, I don't even remember falling into bed I was so exhausted. I am however, a bit nervous for the events today." I watched my hand as my fingers picked at the edge of the table as I thought about the upcoming ceremony.

"I understand your nerves. Today is a big day, not only for you, but all of Ochana. You are the first ever Prince to be introduced at eighteen. Every prince before you was introduced just days after their birth." Sila explained.

"Shouldn't we call it a royal debut then, or a grand ceremony? I mean, coronation to me is so formal. Where I come from, it only happens when a royal is to become a King or a Queen, but I will be staying the same." I reflected.

Sila placed her hand over mine on the table. "Today, you will officially become the Prince of Ochana, a milestone for all that live here. An official ceremony has been written and rewritten many times just for you, just for this day." She squeezed my hand and let go. "When it is over, you will understand why today is much more than just a debut." She winked at me and stood. "Go get ready, I will wait for you in the hall."

I showered and washed up as quickly as I could and threw on an outfit that had appeared on my bed while I was in the shower. I met Sila in the hallway in record time, as I closed the door behind me I could hear a low chuckle come from her. It seemed it would take quite a bit of time for anyone to forget about my little incident with the door.

***

The procession started much like a wedding. As soon as the music started, Meka, who held the Book of Aprella high in the air above her head, followed by the council led the walk down the path that would bring us to the castle steps. Eva and I followed behind them, our hands held tight, Rylan and Sila were behind us and Zane behind them.

As we reached the steps, I watched as Meka trotted to the top with the book still held high. The council stopped at the bottom of the stairs and bowed, then split into two groups as they took their places on the steps below Meka; two to the right and two to the left. Eva and I stopped at the bottom of the steps and bowed as we were instructed to do earlier in the day. Rylan, Sila and Zane stopped behind us to do the same. As I looked up towards Meka and the council, I made note of their robes, each represented the four founding dragons. Allas wore a green robe that represented the Leslos, Luka donned the Sien's signature silver, Jules was draped in a blue robe for the Galians and, lastly, Jericho wore a red robe that represented the Wolands.

Rylan and Sila walked around us and took their spots in the center, halfway up the steps, Zane strode up and stood on the other side of Eva.

Rylan lifted his arms. "Welcome all of Ochana on this momentous day. This day will be marked in our history books as we celebrate the coronation of my son, Prince Colton of Ochana." Rylan exclaimed as the dragons behind us clapped and cheered.

I took my cue and walked forward to ascend the castle steps. I stopped right below Rylan and Sila, head bowed. I prayed no one could see how nervous I was.

"Eighteen years ago you were born to Queen Sila and myself, giving us great joy." Rylan tilted my chin up so I had no choice but to look him in the eye. "With joy came sadness as we handed you over to your human parents, Michael and Ella. We will forever be grateful to them for raising you to be the man you are today. The bond that was created between the three of you will live in your heart for the rest of your life. Use the love you have for them as a light during your journey as a protector." Rylan placed a hand on the top of my head, his other held high in the air as he continued. "Today we offer you the gifts of our four founding dragons, gifts that will reinforce your title as Prince of Ochana and guide you on your passage as our next King, if you so do accept." Rylan removed his hand from my head and stepped away from me.

Luka took Rylan's place in front of me. In his hands, he clutched a golden robe fashioned together with the insignia of each founding dragon. He held the robe out for me, "I offer you this robe, created by the eyes and stitched by the hands of the Siens as a gift and a promise to always stand by your side. This robe represents togetherness and friendship. Do you accept, My Prince?" Luka asked.

"I do." I answered as Luka placed the robe over my shoulders and walked back to his spot.

Jules stepped down next and stood in front of me, holding out a scepter; on the end of it four dragon heads with one of the largest gems I had ever seen held between them. "My Prince, I offer you this scepter to represent power and wealth. The Galians handpicked the diamond from the royal hoard to be placed between the four founding dragons. This scepter represents our everlasting bond and commitment to each other. Do you accept our gift, My Prince?" Jules asked.

"I do." I responded as I took hold of the scepter with my right hand.

Jericho stood in front of me next. He held out a sword enclosed within a scabbard. "My Prince, it is with honor that I offer you this gift representing strength and courage." He pulled the sword out of its scabbard and held it high. "This sword was created with the strongest of graphene and the fire of Woland. Do you accept this gift?" He asked with his head bowed.

"I do." I replied as Jericho place the scabbard over my head, which placed the sword by my left hip.

Allas joined me next; she stood in front of me with a crown held out in front of her. The crown was a single layer of gems. "My Prince, I offer you this crown to represent knowledge and leadership. This crown was crafted with four precious jewels to represent our four founding dragons. The emeralds represent the Leslos, the rubies the Wolands, the sapphires the Galians and the obsidians represent the Siens. These four gems are welded together using dragon fire. Do you accept our gift?"

"I do." I responded as she placed the crown over the top of my head, it rested just above my ears.

Rylan returned to his position in front of me. "It is an honor to introduce to all, my son, Prince Colton of Ochana." Rylan announced as he turned me to face the dragons below.

It was my first real glimpse of all of Ochana, it seemed every dragon was here to witness my coronation. Each dragon clapped and cheered as they took me in donning the gifts I just accepted. Rylan's voice brought me back to his attention as he turned me back around to face him.

"Not only today do we acknowledge your birthright as Prince of Ochana, but we acknowledge your right as the Keeper of Dragons." Rylan stated.

"I ask that your other half join us, as you both take your oath as such."

Eva climbed up the steps and stood to the right of me. She was wearing a beautiful gold dress that sparkled as it flowed behind her. The gown was custom created by a group of Siens to signify Eva's role as the golden dragon.

Rylan placed one hand on my head and the other on Eva's, he then tilted his head up towards the sky as he spoke. "The Keeper of Dragons have been gifted to us by our mother Aprella. We accept her gift with open hearts and fierce protection." The crowd behind us echoed Rylan's last words.

He looked down to us, his eyes glowing a bright green. "I offer you my protection as you lead us out of this time of fear." Again, all of Ochana repeated his words.

"Do you, the Keeper of Dragon's accept our gift?" Rylan asked.

Eva's hand found mine as we spoke together, "We do."

Rylan's hands fell from our heads as we turned to face the dragons of Ochana. Everyone clapped and cheered. Music started to play and many dragons began to dance along the grassy grounds that surrounded the castle. I watched as a few shifted and blew their dragonic breathing fire into the air to demonstrate their excitement.

"Wherever you lead them, they will follow." Rylan whispered in my ear as he passed by to lead our procession back through the streets of Ochana. "Our trust lies with the two of you."

My future was full of unknowns and I knew the constant threats would continue to be placed on my shoulders. I didn't know what the future held or how it would turn out. But one thing I knew for sure, as long as I had Eva and my new family by my side, I would fight.

* * *

Continue the Keeper of Dragons Series in book two, The Elven Alliance

https://www.amazon.com/dp/B01N01MBLF/

J.A. Culican

Books by J.A. Culican

Book 1: Keeper of Dragons – The Prince Returns

Book 2: Keeper of Dragons – The Elven Alliance

The fates have spoken.

Cole and Eva are the Keeper of Dragons - the only ones who can save all true beings from a time of fear.

Uncontrollable power.

Cole finds himself unstable, unpredictable and volatile. He has no control of the tilium-fairy magic he stole from the farros. Out of options, the dragons turn to a once ally - the elves - for help. Curious about the dragon who wields both dragon and fairy magic, they accept -but on their terms only. The dragons must submit to Prince Gaber and his rules.

A new enemy.

Queen Tana continues to haunt Cole's dreams, as a new enemy shows his face - another fallen enemy with a bigger agenda than the farros-fallen fairies; an enemy stronger and smarter; an enemy with an army that could destroy all true beings. Enter King Eldrick of the eldens-the fallen elves.

J.A. Culican

Book 1: Second Sight - Hollows Ground

What if you could foresee death?

Mirela can prophesy the death of whomever she sees. At thirteen, Ela foretold the death of her best friend, only to watch it happen before her very eyes. Ela, now twenty-one, spends her days locked away in her apartment, avoiding the public and the gift she considers a curse.

Until he appears.

Luka Conway is handsome. Charming. And magical. After Ela predicts yet another death, Luka leads her to an underground city hidden beneath Atlanta, populated by empaths, telepaths, and seers. Luka is a Shade, a soldier fighting a secret war against the Wraiths, a deadly group of sorcerers who wish to take over the world. Ela is given no choice; she must prove herself a Shade, and use her powers for the light, or she will be put to death. Resolved to her fate, Ela trains as a warrior, determined to put her curse to good use. Then Talon Michaels appears. He's just as dashing as Luka, and even more dangerous. A Wraith, Talon warns Ela that the Shades aren't all what they appear. Who can Ela trust, if anyone? Should her powers be used for good...or evil?

Coming Fall 2017

J.A. Culican

About the author

About J.A. Culican

J.A. Culican is a teacher by day and a writer by night. She lives in New Jersey with her husband of eleven years and their four young children. She spends her evenings at home, with her family, watching Harry Potter and Star Wars. When not home you can find her at the soccer or field hockey fields, rooting her children on.

J.A. Culican's inspiration to start writing came from her children and their love for all things magical. Bedtime stories turned to reality after her oldest daughter begged her for the book from which her stories of dragons came from. In turn, the series, Keeper of Dragons was born.

J.A. Culican

Contact me

I can't wait to hear from you!

Email:
jaculican@gmail.com

Website:
http://jaculican.com

Facebook Author Page:
https://www.facebook.com/jaculican

Amazon Author Page:
http://amazon.com/author/jaculican

Twitter:
https://twitter.com/jaculican

Instagram:
http://instagram.com/jaculican

Pinterest:
http://pinterest.com/jaculican

Add me on Goodreads here:
https://www.goodreads.com/author/show/15287808.J_A_C
ulican

J.A. Culican

The Prince Returns